STALKED BY A KILLER

Ten minutes later, Fran was making her way back from the teachers' lounge. Like Miss Merriwether's phone, the teachers' phone was locked. She was halfway down the first floor hallway when she heard the footsteps.

She turned sharply.

There was nothing in the hall, nothing but lockers, all of them shut.

"Mike?" she called.

Silence.

"Owen? Jill?"

Feeling foolish, she turned and continued walking.

But now she was sure of it, sure she was not alone. She stopped, listening hard. She heard a door scrape on its hinges.

"Jaclyn?" she called. "Glen?"

Her heart was pounding. Look at me, she thought. Scared silly. And of what?

She turned around again. Keeping her eyes on the long dark hallway, she started walking backward.

No one jumped out at her from the dark classroom doorways. No demons popped out of the lockers to grab her in their claws.

C'mon, she told herself as she reached the end of the hall. Get a grip, Weber!

She was still walking backward when she felt the body smack into her, the arms close around her.

Fran screamed.

BOOK YOUR PLACE ON OUR WEBSITE AND MAKE THE READING CONNECTION!

We've created a customized website just for our very special readers, where you can get the inside scoop on everything that's going on with Zebra, Pinnacle and Kensington books.

When you come online, you'll have the exciting opportunity to:

- View covers of upcoming books
- Read sample chapters
- Learn about our future publishing schedule (listed by publication month *and author*)
- Find out when your favorite authors will be visiting a city near you
- Search for and order backlist books from our online catalog
- Check out author bios and background information
- Send e-mail to your favorite authors
- Meet the Kensington staff online
- Join us in weekly chats with authors, readers and other guests
- Get writing guidelines
- AND MUCH MORE!

**Visit our website at
http://www.pinnaclebooks.com**

DEADLY DETENTION

ERIC WEINER

PINNACLE BOOKS
KENSINGTON PUBLISHING CORP.
www.pinnaclebooks.com

PINNACLE BOOKS are published by

Kensington Publishing Corp.
850 Third Avenue
New York, NY 10022

Copyright © 1994 by Eric Weiner

All rights reserved. No part of this book may be reproduced in any form or by any means without the prior written consent of the Publisher, excepting brief quotes used in reviews.

If you purchased this book without a cover, you should be aware that this book is stolen property. It was reported as "unsold and destroyed" to the Publisher and neither the Author nor the Publisher has received any payment for this "stripped book."

Pinnacle and the P logo are trademarks of Kensington Publishing Corp.

First Printing: June, 1994
First Pinnacle Printing: September, 2000

Printed in the United States of America
10 9 8 7 6 5 4 3 2

One

It was quarter to four on a cold December afternoon.

Classroom #301 sat empty.

Waiting.

Then the door swung open sharply. A pretty seventeen-year-old girl stuck her head inside, her ice-blue eyes coolly surveying the room.

Like every other room at Harrison High, Classroom #301 was drab. Five rows of battered desk chairs faced the gray metal teacher's desk. A few posters decorated the walls, their edges curling. Dust motes danced dully in the beams of fading sunlight.

The girl turned and called back into the hall. "Glen? C'mon! We're the first ones."

She dumped her books on the arm of a desk chair in the front row. Sat down. Got up again. Normally, Jaclyn loved to sit in the front row, especially for classes with male teachers. Her short skirts drove them wild. But this was detention, she reminded herself. The less attention she got, the better.

Detention. Kids hated it even more than trips to the principal's office. But Jaclyn wasn't feeling glum. She was feeling keyed up, excited. She'd never had detention before in her life.

She shifted to a seat in the middle of the second row. Her short, ultrabright vinyl skirt crinkled noisily each time she moved. "Glen!" she called again.

She had left the classroom door wide open. In walked a tall seventeen-year-old boy carrying a large pile of books under one arm. His handsome face was blank—and wary. He stayed near the door. "This is so ridiculous," he said. "I mean, I'm missing basketball practice for this."

Thanks to his grace in all athletic games and his almost movie-star good looks, Jaclyn's boyfriend was one of the most popular kids at Harrison High. As far as Jaclyn was concerned, though, he was also stupid. She stopped chewing her wad of gum and tilted her pretty little chin downward as she gave him a look of exaggerated surprise. "You're missing practice? Gee. What a great point, Glen. When the detention monitor arrives, why don't you just explain that to him?"

She reached inside her orange varsity cheerleading jacket and pulled out two tiny earphones, which she slipped into her ears. With a toss of her head, she hid the earphones be-

DEADLY DETENTION

hind her hair. Then she pressed the sleeve of her jacket. There was a tiny click. Hidden inside the jacket's arm was an Aiwa walkman, which she had just turned on. She started nodding her head back and forth to the music. She shut her eyes.

Sometimes, with guys like Glen, the best strategy was just to ignore them.

She's ignoring me, Glen thought with disbelief. And the next thought was one that had been going through his head for weeks. Why was he still going out with her?

Jaclyn kept tossing her head to the music. She swayed sexily. She gave a little moan, and Glen remembered why he was still going out with her.

He dropped his books on a desk and crossed to the window. Classroom #301 was on the third and top floor of Harrison High. Still, the windows didn't afford much of a view. Last year all the windows at Harrison had been covered with a thick wire mesh.

Glen really couldn't blame them for doing it. For years, kids had been sneaking over to the school grounds late at night and pelting the windows with rocks. He had done it himself, more than once.

Glen peered out through the grimy glass and wire mesh. The sky was gray. Down below he could see part of the lawn; it was covered with slushy snow. He could also see the black macadam parking lot. There was plenty of activity going on down there. Kids were shouting to each other, slamming their car doors. They were so happy to be out of this place for another day. Glen sighed again, more deeply this time. There were butterflies in his stomach, like before a big game.

Still looking out the window, he muttered, "This place is like a prison."

"What?"

"I said"—Glen turned from the window, and remembering Jaclyn's walkman, raised his voice several decibels—"I said this place is like a prison!"

Jaclyn clicked off her tape player. Then she crossed and uncrossed her legs. Her shimmery black tights made a swish sound that made Glen's heart thump. He couldn't help it. That swish sound excited him more than the swish he heard after taking a perfect shot in a basketball game.

Jaclyn said, "Come here."

Glen stared at her, his mouth slack. As he watched, she removed a large wad of green sugarless gum and stuck it under her desk. "I said come here."

"Why?"

"Why do you think?"

DEADLY DETENTION 9

Glen didn't move. "What about this afternoon? I thought you said—"

"I told you to forget that."

Glen hesitated. "People will be here any second."

"No they won't." Jaclyn nodded up at the old wall clock. "We're early. We're the only fools who rushed to detention."

Shrugging his shoulders, Glen walked slowly down her row, slumping into the seat next to hers. When he put his books down, she took his hand. She held his fingers up to her face, sniffing them as if they were a bouquet of roses. Then she bit the tip of his forefinger so hard he yelped.

"Are you crazy?" he demanded.

"I wanted to get your attention."

"Well you got it!"

He tried to pull his hand away, but she held on to it. Smiling, her white teeth glistening, she now started to move his hand slowly down from her mouth. Down past the silver peace-sign medallion which hung around her neck on a thin, black shoestring. Down past the open collar of her cheerleading jacket. Down.

Glen jerked his hand away. "Jaclyn," he said huskily. "C'mon, this is what got us into trouble in the first place."

"So?"

He shrugged. "So we gotta act like we learned our lesson, at least for one hour."

Jaclyn's ice-blue eyes looked even icier than usual. "You're a bore," she said.

"Jaclyn—"

But he didn't get any further in pleading his case. Because just then Jill Berman, another senior, trudged into the room.

Jill was a tall girl with shoulder-length auburn hair that hung down limply around her head like something that had died. She had freckles and thick eyebrows that grew together a little bit behind her glasses. Her oily skin always had a slight sheen to it. And as if she wasn't burdened with enough problems, she was also fat.

What a sad case. Glen gave her his best smile. The truth was, he was glad to have the interruption.

Jill Berman stopped short as she entered the classroom. She was sure she was interrupting. It didn't seem right that the cheerleader and the basketball star would be in detention. "Oh, sorry," Jill said, peering at them through her thick glasses. "Uh . . . is this the right room?"

"Yup," Jaclyn said, studying her glossy red nails. "Overeaters Anonymous."

Jill laughed good-naturedly, her shoulders

going up and down. She loved a good joke, even at her own expense. "You know, I actually do go to O.A.," she said. "Every Friday afternoon."

"No kidding," Jaclyn said.

"Yeah," Jill said. She smiled broadly. "I'm a card-carrying member. But isn't it funny they call it Overeaters *Anonymous?* Like no one knows I overeat, right?"

Guffawing at her own joke, Jill moved to the nearest chair and sat down, squeezing her legs under the arm of the desk. She grunted. It wasn't easy stuffing herself into the small space. They made such a fuss ev-erywhere about making buildings accessible for handicapped people. They added ramps and elevators for people in wheelchairs. You would think they would do something for fat people, she thought bitterly. But no.

Turning in her seat—again with difficulty—Jill smiled at Jaclyn and Glen. Only Glen smiled back. There was an awkward silence.

Jill hated silence. She always felt compelled to fill it, just like she felt compelled to fill her stomach. "I've never had detention before," she said.

"Me neither," Jaclyn said, in a tone that seemed designed to end any further discussion. The cheerleader turned away.

More silence. "I hope they serve snacks," Jill said.

Neither Jaclyn nor Glen answered. Jill looked at the large wall clock, then at her watch. She groaned. Her watch was fifteen minutes slow.

The watch, with its goofy Bart Simpson face and its pink leather band, had been a Christmas present from her mom, two years ago. Jill took it off her wrist and started carefully resetting the time. "This watch is always running slow," she said, "but I love it so much I can't bear to stop wearing it."

No one responded. There was tension in the room. Jill could feel it. She always felt tense waiting for a teacher. But this was worse. This was detention. Though Jill was trying to stay calm, or at least *look* calm, her stomach was already churning.

She studied Bart Simpson's yellow face. If only she could change time by setting the watch. She'd set it to five and this would all be over.

When she looked up, Glen was smiling at her, which made her feel a little better. "So what are you in for?" he asked.

"Child molestation," she answered. She giggled. "No, but seriously folks, Mrs. Howard caught me smoking in the bathroom. And speaking of cigarettes—God! I could really use one right now."

She opened her black drawstring bag and fumbled inside. She produced a jar of Stridex medicated buff pads, which she tossed back quickly, hoping Jaclyn and Glen hadn't seen it. Fumbling some more, she pulled out two empty bags of Reese's Pieces and then a half-eaten jumbo bag of peanut M&Ms. She held the bag of candy toward Jaclyn and Glen. "Want one?"

Jaclyn disdainfully eyed the candy, arching one blond eyebrow. "No thanks."

Jill started popping two candies into her mouth at a time. "I'm so glad they started making the red ones again, aren't you guys? Even if they are carcinogenic."

"You shouldn't eat so much," Glen said, but he didn't say it meanly.

"You're right," agreed Jill. "The thing is, I'm really nervous about all this weight I've been gaining"—she popped another candy into her mouth and chewed noisily—"and junk food is the only thing that calms me down."

"Better be careful, Jill," said a voice at the door. "The green ones make you horny as hell."

"Mike Morricone!" exclaimed Jill gleefully. "Fancy meeting you here."

The junior strolling into the classroom was on the stocky side, with the powerful arms you might expect from a wrestler, which he was. He wore a purple Harrison High T-shirt, tight because of his many muscles, and a backward white cap. He was smiling his usual twinkly-eyed, close-mouthed smile. He stopped at Jill's desk. "So you got detention, too? High-five!"

They high-fived loudly. All right, Jill was thinking, Mike Morricone! Things were looking up. Mike was Jill's definition of a fun-loving guy. The guy never had a care on his mind.

Trying not to grit his teeth or show how upset he was, Mike swung into a seat right behind the heavy girl's. He couldn't even look in Jaclyn's direction. He just nodded at the other two students—"Glen, Jaclyn." Then, smiling more broadly, he reached over to pat Jill affectionately on the back. "So, Berman, whadja do this time?"

"Oh, right, like I usually get detention," Jill said, laughing. She reached under her sweater and produced a pack of Virginia Slims, which she held up by way of explanation.

Mike's eyes went wide with surprise. "Since when you do smoke?"

"Since I started doing my college applications."

Mike laughed. But what he was thinking was how sorry he felt for her. The heavy girl was looking even more nervous—and fat—than

DEADLY DETENTION 15

usual. And now she was smoking. "You ought to relax, Berman," he told her. "Believe me—you don't have to worry about getting into a good school."

"That's what you say. I'm so wired I can barely sleep at night."

"Look, what difference does it make, anyway?" he asked, grinning. "That's what you have to ask yourself. School, college, grades—what's the difference? It's all a big joke."

"Some joke," Jill said.

"Here," Mike said, taking the cigarettes. "I'll help you quit."

She grabbed for the pack. "No way."

Mike laughed. "Just teasin' ya." He two-fingered a cigarette from the pack and slipped it behind his ear, then handed the rest back.

"What about you? How'd you get detention?" Jill asked him. "Wait a minute. Don't tell me. Let me guess. You farted really loudly in homeroom?"

Mike smiled proudly. His farting abilities were legendary at Harrison. As well they should be. He had once ripped off a doozy in assembly, right in the middle of a speech by Harrison's mayor, Mr. Hartley.

Mr. Hartley had been droning on for twenty minutes about the importance of scholarship. Harrison wasn't a rich town, said Hartley. Not like some of those fancy-pants

Bergen County towns that were closer to Manhattan, such as Englewood and Mont-clair. No, said Hartley, Harrison wasn't rich at all. *But*—he waved a finger in the air—Harrison High was still famous. Famous for the quality of its teachers and famous for its long tradition of academic excellence. Why, for years the students of Harrison had proven that money wasn't everything. With diligence and hard work—

And right then Mike had farted so long and so loudly that he got detention for a week. Worth every minute, too.

"Nope," Mike now told Jill. "Didn't fart. Guess again."

"Okay." Jill thought a moment. "You made fun of Mrs. Walker!"

Mrs. Walker was the school nurse. She walked ramrod straight, and Mike loved to walk right behind her in the hallways, imitating her perfectly.

"Nope," Mike said. "It wasn't Mrs. Walker this time." He leaned back, two hands behind his head. "This time it wasn't my fault at all. My car wouldn't start. I didn't get here until after third period."

Jill cackled. "Right."

"I know, sounds like a dumb excuse, right?"

"Right," agreed Jaclyn, clicking her walkman back on.

Ignoring Jaclyn's comment, Mike sat up, his

DEADLY DETENTION 17

arms spread wide. "Jill, I swear to God, that's what happened. Wake up this morning, the car is dead. Turn the key. Nothing. I don't mean, you know, a little sound like someday it might turn over. Silence. Not even a click."

"Maybe it's the weather," Glen offered.

"Right," Mike said curtly. " 'Course," he continued to Jill, "I wasn't too broken up about it. When I found out it wouldn't start, I called Triple-A and went right back to bed. I figured it's like a snow day. I was going to watch the game shows all day."

"All right!" exclaimed Jill. Then she frowned. "So what are you doing here?"

"Triple-A shows up at eleven, right before 'Wheel of Fortune.' All I got to see was cartoons. *And* I got detention."

Mike turned to the dirty-blond cheerleader a few seats away. He waited until she turned the tape back off, then asked, "Since when do they punish Miss Popular?"

Jaclyn made a face and tossed her perfect head of hair, as if to say, "Funny." What she really said was, "Miss Johnson caught us in the music room at lunch. Doing you know what."

Mike grinned, but humorlessly. He knew what.

"Why do you have to tell everybody about it?" Glen asked sullenly.

Jaclyn's head jerked in her boyfriend's direction. "Why? You ashamed?"

"No," Glen said quickly. "It's just—" He looked away. In a lower voice, he finished lamely, "I don't see why you have to tell everybody."

Jaclyn shook her head. "I don't like the way you're acting, you know that?" She pressed her sleeve and clicked her walkman on again, disappearing rapidly into the music. She lolled her perfect head back, made little fists over her head and stretched kittenishly. She closed her eyes. And then she ran her pink tongue around her lips, moistening them slowly, so slowly.

Mike, who was still watching her, winced and said, "Ouch!"

This is going to be hell, he told himself. He turned back to Jill. "So who's covering detention today?"

"Well," Jill said, looking around the dingy classroom. "This is usually Mr. Osmond's room. So I'm praying it's him."

With his white hair and bony body, Mr. Osmond looked like he was about eighty years old. He was not too strong on discipline, as you could tell by the amount of graffiti scrawled on the desks. In places where kids had pushed their desks up to the sides of the room, there was even graffiti on the walls.

Mike himself had added his fair share over the years.

He placed his hands together in fake prayer. "Please, God, let it be Osmond, let it be Osmond."

Glen said, "Osmond was out sick today."

"Thanks a lot, God," said Mike.

"Just as long as it's not Crowley," said Jaclyn, who had turned off her walkman yet again.

At the sound of Crowley's name, Mike's stomach—which was already tense—tensed up even more. Apparently the name had the same magical effect on all the students. All heads turned toward the cheerleader.

"Why would it be Crowley?" Glen asked, nervously running his hand through his short brown hair.

Jaclyn said, "It just could be, that's all."

"She's right. They rotate detention duty," Mike said.

"Thank you, detention expert," Jaclyn told Mike. Her voice was sugary with sarcasm. To Glen and Jill, she said, "The list is posted in the principal's office. I was in there today but I didn't see whether today is Crowley's day or not."

"Oh, my God," said Jill. "Perish the thought." She started popping three M&Ms at a time.

"The Corporal for detention?" Glen said,

shaking his head. He chuckled. "Hey—that'd be corporal punishment."

No one laughed. For a moment, everyone in the room sat silently. The Corporal, thought Mike. He shuddered.

Mr. Lance Crowley (or "the Corporal," as students called him behind his back) was Harrison's biology teacher. Among parents and teachers, he had built up a reputation for being a tough, but superb educator. Last year he'd even been written up in *The Bergen Record*. The article had talked about Crowley's bootcamp approach to education and science, but it had made it all sound like a joke, like something the students thought was fun. The article also pointed out that Crowley's science club had produced two Westinghouse scholars. The article said he was beloved by parents and students alike.

Well, the newspaper story got it half right, thought Mike. The parents *did* love Crowley. The students—well, the students were a different story. The students had always been petrified. And the last couple of months . . .

"The guy was always strict," Glen said, "but lately . . . Sheesh!"

"I think the man is really flipping out," Jill agreed. "You should have heard him in class today. Betsy Doyle refused to pith her frog? Said it was cruelty to animals? So Crowley starts screaming at her. I mean, screaming his head off. He got his face right into hers, too, you know the way he does. Like a drill sergeant."

"Drill *corporal*," Mike corrected.

"He was in the Marines," Glen said.

"Duh," said Jaclyn. Putting a hand up to the side of her mouth in a fake attempt at secrecy, she added, "He's got a drinking problem."

"Tell me about it," said Jill. "It's gotten so I can smell it from three rows back."

Jaclyn frowned at Jill, then said, "You know about the dartboard?" Jill shook her head, wide-eyed. "He's got this dartboard in the teachers' lounge. And he cuts out pictures from the yearbook of kids he doesn't like? And he tapes them right over the bull's-eye."

"That's a lie," Mike said. He tried to say it casually, to make sure Jaclyn didn't think he was scared.

"I swear." Jaclyn leaned forward, beckoning Mike and Jill toward her with the crook of a pretty finger. She lowered her voice to a stage whisper. "Get this. Crowley's son is like this total druggie."

"Oh, everyone knows that," Jill said matter-of-factly. "His son's been arrested twice for possession."

"I know," Jaclyn continued smoothly, "but

did you know—" She paused for dramatic effect.

"Know what?" Glen asked.

Jaclyn grinned. "His wife is so upset about their son that she's had this complete nervous breakdown thing where she's like afraid to go out of the house."

"No! Where did you hear that?" Jill asked, her jaw dropping.

"It's bull," Mike said.

"How do you know?" Jaclyn asked. Her blue eyes flashed.

Mike shrugged. "How do *you* know, that's the question."

Jaclyn curled her upper lip in a sneer. "My mother used to play doubles with Mrs. Crowley, okay? Last summer Mrs. C dropped out of the game and wouldn't give a reason. And when my mom finally spoke to Mr. Crowley about it, all he would say was that she *wasn't well*. Then she found out the true story from one of his neighbors, who she plays bridge with? Mrs. C had a nervous breakdown, I'm telling you."

The four students sat in silence a moment. "Well, it's not too surprising," Jill said at last. "*I'd* have a nervous breakdown if I was married to the guy."

"And I'd do drugs if I was his son," added Mike. "Hey, I do them anyway!"

Jaclyn bit off the cap of her black Bic. Pressing down hard, she started scrawling the pen back and forth on her desktop, darkening an already heavily-inked groove in the wood. She kept her head down. "It's all because of the son," she said. "It's because of the son doing drugs that the mother broke down. Because she's so disappointed in him. And my mom says that's why Crowley's been so mean to all his students lately. It's because of what his son did. Now Crowley hates *all* kids. It's like he wants . . . revenge."

"Wow," Jill said. "That's awful."

They were all silent, listening to the clock tick. Then the old radiators started their eerie knocking.

"You don't think we're going to get Crowley, do you?" Jill asked.

No one answered.

Tick, tick, tick . . .

"Now I'm really getting nervous," Jill said. "Somebody tell me I shouldn't be nervous, okay? Guys?"

"I don't know," Glen said softly. "If you ask me, the guy's really about to snap. He's like right on the edge. I was there the day he broke that pointer. I really thought he was going to go berserk and start stabbing everyone."

"Okay," Jill said. "That's enough. I'm starting to freak."

"Don't make me keep you after school,"

Jaclyn said, lowering her voice in imitation of Crowley's deep-throated rasp. "Don't make me do it. Because if *you* have to stay late, then *I* have to stay late. And that makes me *mad!*"

Jill gasped, and then laughed and applauded. So did Mike. Just about everyone at Harrison did an imitation of Crowley these days. But Mike had to admit it, Jaclyn's was one of the best.

Jill leaned back in her chair and tapped Mike's powerful shoulder. "Do yours," she begged.

Mike smiled, his eyes crinkling. He was tempted, but—he glanced toward the door. "I better not."

"Aw, go on," Jaclyn said. "You've already got detention. What's the worst that can happen to you?"

Mike thought for a moment. The last thing he wanted was to look like a coward in front of Jaclyn. On the other hand, he'd really be asking for it. He pushed himself up out of the chair. "Okay."

He immediately changed his posture, pushing out his stomach to imitate Crowley's barrel chest and swinging his arms as he walked in the biology teacher's bullying, ape-like manner. He jutted his jaw forward, looking furious. He darted his head from side to side, as if trying to catch the other three students goofing off.

Then he walked behind the teacher's desk

and mimed hoisting a heavy briefcase. He slammed both hands down on the metal desktop, hard, to imitate the way Crowley always dropped his briefcase. "Good morning," he barked. He made a little *tsk* sound, sucking on a tooth.

Everyone applauded. Mike grinned. He knew he had caught Crowley's mannerisms perfectly.

Jill whistled. He spun sharply, pointing right at her, his eyes dark with fury. "You making fun of me, Berman?"

Jill was laughing so hard now there were tears in her eyes. She forced out a "No."

"Don't make me keep you after school," he warned. "Because if you have to stay late, that means that I—"

"MORRICONE!"

The shout came from just outside the open doorway.

Everyone in the room jumped.

All blood drained instantly out of Mike's face.

Crowley!

Two

"You *dare* to imitate *me?*" Crowley shouted. "I'll *kill* you. You hear me? I'll kill you!"

"Oh, God," mumbled Mike.

But his voice was filled with relief.

Because Crowley was rushing into the room now, and Mike could see that it wasn't really Crowley at all. It was Owen Lasker.

Owen was a short, skinny senior with a persistent case of tiny pimples that gave his forehead and cheeks the consistency of a Nestle's Crunch Bar. He was wearing his usual attempt at cool clothes—a black sweater with no T-shirt underneath and black shades that looked ridiculous perched on his bulbous nose. He had a high voice, too, to go along with his nerdy appearance, but just now he had managed to imitate Crowley's low growl beautifully.

The skinny teenager stopped in front of the teacher's desk, giggling his high-pitched laugh. His thumbs were hooked nervously over his jean's front pockets. He laughed so hard he coughed.

DEADLY DETENTION 27

Mike nodded appreciatively. "You got me, man."

Poor Owen. He was pretty much a total freak as far as the student body was concerned. He got teased, picked on, chased, attacked—you name it. Well, at least—thought Mike—at least Owen still had a sense of humor.

All the time he was laughing, Owen kept thinking bitterly, I did it! I did it! I fooled them all!

Jill was clutching her chest. "I swallowed three M&Ms whole."

"You moron," Jaclyn told Owen. "You could have given us all a heart attack."

"Ha-ha!" Owen said, grinning at her. He couldn't contain his glee. He felt as if his grin might just keep spreading until his whole face turned inside out. "That was the best," he complimented himself. "The best!"

He sat down in the front row, then swiveled to look back at the other students. "Hey, Glen," he called. "What'd you get on your calculus quiz?"

Glen rocked back on his chair, smiling. That guy, thought Owen. He thought he was so cool. Just because he looked like one of those hunks you saw on swimsuit calendars. Owen would have killed to look like that. It made him hate Glen all the more.

"I got a ninety-nine," Glen said.

Owen whistled. He pretended to be impressed. "Wow, not bad."

C'mon, he thought. Ask me. *Ask me.*

Nobody asked him.

"Hey, you know what?" said Owen. "You *almost* beat me." He could feel his nervous smile spreading across his face again.

"Oh, yeah?" Glen asked. So casual. Like he didn't care.

"Yeah. Uh, I got a hundred," Owen said. He tried to sound just as casual as Glen, but it didn't work.

"*Only* a hundred?" Mike asked. He sat down in the back row. "Lasker, you're slipping."

Owen giggled. "I guess you're right. No extra credit."

Jaclyn took out an emery board and started filing her long, glossy red nails. The girl was so sexy and pretty, it actually gave Owen a pain in the gut to look at her. Like if he looked at her too long, he'd get a bleeding ulcer. He looked away quickly.

Jaclyn said, "Wow, Owen, that's really impressive. I have like a completely different picture of you now. Like a he-man or something."

The words stung. Behind his dark shades, Owen's eyes blinked rapidly. "I don't mind being smarter than you, if that—if that's what you're saying," he told her.

"Well, I got a hundred, too, if *that's* what you're saying," Jaclyn said, ever so calmly.

Owen felt a stab of pain. She had tied him! How humiliating! To be tied by a cheerleader!

"Hi, guys," said a sweet and familiar voice from the door.

Senior Fran Weber walked into the room, scuffing her saddle shoes across the cement floor. Owen turned to look at her. He was surprised to see her—and instantly glad, too. The sight of Frannie was like a soothing lotion on his wounded ego.

Fran was a tall and pretty girl, with apple cheeks and dark bangs that hung down to her kind green eyes. Right now she was wearing a scalloped black lace top and a black skirt with white buttons up the front. Somehow, the blackness of her outfit did nothing to diminish her sunny air.

Jill Berman took the words right out of Owen's mouth. "Now I've seen everything," she said as Fran closed the door behind her. "Frannie Weber's got detention?"

Fran nodded her head in acknowledgment, giving Jill a rueful grin. It *was* a strange feeling, she had to admit. She sat down, took her black backpack off her shoulder, and dropped it on the floor with a thud. "It wasn't my fault," she said, "believe me."

"What happened?" Glen asked.

She turned her palms up to show that she didn't know, the gesture jangling her three bracelets. "It was so dumb," she told the group. "I guess somebody must have framed me. You know, like as a practical joke or something."

"She stole Beth Corn's wallet," Jaclyn corrected.

Fran's eyes widened with shock. She shook her head. "I didn't," she said simply.

"Second period, advanced English," said Jaclyn, tossing her head so that her hair whipped. "Beth Corn comes in crying. Says she went to the cafeteria to buy a bag of Bugles and found her wallet missing." Jaclyn was giggling now, warming to her story. "So then Miss Mack makes everyone open up their desks and bags and—"

Jaclyn was laughing so hard she had trouble going on. The laughter sounded fake.

"So guess where the wallet is?" Jaclyn asked. "Right in Fran's backpack."

"Wow, that really *is* funny," Mike said without smiling.

Good old Mike, thought Fran. To Jaclyn, she said, "I didn't do it. I mean, why would I take Beth Corn's wallet?"

"For the money," Jaclyn answered, and cackled. "Guys, I'm telling you, it was so funny. Can you picture it? Miss Mack accusing her number one teacher's pet of stealing? If you'd have been there, you would have busted a gut."

"Oh, I'm *sure*," said Jill. She sounded as if she were trying to sound sarcastic, but she couldn't really pull it off.

"I'm telling you," Fran said. "Somebody planted the wallet there."

"Hmm ... I wonder who," Mike said. He glanced meaningfully at Jaclyn.

The blond girl pursed her red lips and blew Mike a kiss. Then she burst into another fit of giggles.

Fran eyed Jaclyn closely. She had always gotten along well with other kids, but Jaclyn had a tendency to test that ability. "Did *you* do it?" Fran demanded.

"Oh, right," said Jaclyn, smiling happily, "like I would tell you if I did."

"You did it, didn't you?" Fran repeated. Jaclyn didn't answer. "Thanks a lot!"

"You're welcome."

Fran felt her cheeks getting red. "Why? I don't get it. I mean, what do you have against me?"

Instead of answering, Jaclyn took out her calculus book and started studying, as if she hadn't even heard her question.

"Don't worry about it, Frannie," Jill said.

"Besides, I gotta say, I'm really glad to see you. I've never had detention before, either. So this way, you can keep me company. You know. Kind of hold my hand a little bit."

Fran laughed. "You got it."

"Hey," said Mike. "Chill out, guys. I have detention all the time. It's not so bad."

Fran glanced around the barren room. "What do you do in detention, anyway?"

Mike said, "Oh, you know, they give you a little busy work, make you sit quietly."

"Can you study?" Owen asked. He was tapping his left sneaker nervously. "I've got my chem final tomorrow."

"Of course you can study," Mike said. "Haven't you noticed? That's all they ever want you to do around this hellhole."

"I've had detention before," Glen said to Fran. "It's a piece of cake."

"Yeah, sure," Jaclyn quickly added, "it'll be fine as long as we don't get—"

The rest of the students finished the sentence together. "Crowley."

"Oh, no," Fran said, covering her mouth. She laughed. "It never even occurred to me. They—they wouldn't leave him alone with us, would they?"

Mike laughed. "They let him out of the asylum, didn't they?"

"Don't laugh," Jaclyn said. "I saw his file."

"What?" gasped Jill. "You mean, like his personnel file?"

"No, his *nail* file." Jaclyn shook her head as if she couldn't believe how stupid some people could be.

"When was this?" Mike asked, looking doubtful.

"When I was in the principal's office," said Jaclyn. "They wanted to talk to me about the winter carnival and stuff. So then Mr. Franklin gets called out of his office and says he'll be right back. And . . . it was sitting right on his desk."

"Did you look at it?" Glen asked.

Jaclyn didn't respond, but her stare was withering. "Anyway," she said, "get this. Before Crowley came here, eight years ago? He was kicked out of his job. Why? Because—this is so unbelievable!—he threw an eraser at a kid who was sleeping in class."

"I've seen him do that," Fran said, shaking her head at the memory. Robert McBride, her sophomore year. He'd burst into tears. It was awful.

"Yeah, well, this time he caught the kid flush in the face," Jaclyn said. "And the kid was wearing glasses, and the glasses broke. This shard of glass got embedded in the kid's cheek."

There was an awed silence.

"So then Harrison High picks him up,"

Owen said in his high voice. "Typical. We get all the crazies."

Owen was right, thought Fran. She thought about Mr. Millman, the calculus teacher. He kept two rabbits in his classroom—Einstein and Freud—which he sang to at the start of each period.

Or there was Ms. Fletcher, who taught physics, and who was so absent-minded she sometimes answered the homeroom phone when the bell rang to end the period.

But Crowley . . .

Crowley was in a class by himself.

"I wonder how bad it would be to have detention with him?" Fran murmured. She glanced at Mike. "Have you ever?"

"Had detention with Crowley? Nope, haven't had the privilege. But personally, I'd rather lie down in front of a Mack truck."

"Maybe we should just split," Jill suggested nervously.

"Not show up for detention?" Jaclyn asked. "We'd only get automatic suspensions, genius."

"She's right," said Owen, his voice cracking. He started beating a bongo beat on his desk.

"Besides," Jaclyn pointed out, "it's not even four yet. We can't even claim he was late."

Fran looked up at the round, black-framed wall clock. Jaclyn was right. The clock's long black minute hand showed one minute to four.

"Someone's coming," Jaclyn said.

Owen stopped drumming. He swallowed loudly.

For a moment, everyone in the room was silent. Fran could hear the steam hissing in the radiators, the tick-tick-tick of the clock.

Then—in the far distance—a door slammed.

She strained her ears.

She heard footsteps approaching.

Click. The clock's long minute hand jerked forward. It pointed straight up to twelve. It was four o'clock.

BANG! The door to Classroom #301 flew open.

Mr. Crowley stood in the doorway, smiling at them—an awful, wolfish grin. "Good afternoon, kiddies!"

Three

The large man made a little *tsk* sound as he sucked on a tooth. Then he carried his heavy, metal-edged black briefcase over to the teacher's desk. He let the bag drop to the floor with a terrible bang. He stared out at the students, just staring, staring and waiting, as if daring a response. One by one—as he stared at each student—they lowered their eyes.

He looked at Fran last. She tried to meet his gaze but couldn't. *He really is like a killer,* was the thought that raced through her mind. She shivered.

Mr. Crowley made that *tsk* sound again.

He was a large man with powerful, hairy arms that looked like they should be tattooed, but weren't. Right now his arms were crossed over his chest, which made his muscles and veins bulge even more. He was wearing a black tie and a white short-sleeved shirt with an ink-stained, pen-filled pocket. His suit pants were a greasy gray. The gray suit and black tie were

DEADLY DETENTION

Crowley's own personal school uniform and looked almost slept in, he had worn them so often.

The teacher shook his head and chuckled. It wasn't a pleasant chuckle. "You wouldn't listen, would you?"

Crowley smiled in a sickening way. "I warned you, didn't I? I warned you not to make me stay after school."

Mr. Crowley sat on the edge of the desk, still staring them down. "So now I have to hang around this crummy school, twiddling my thumbs, because *you,*"—he pointed at Owen—"and you"—he pointed at Jill—"couldn't behave yourself for one single lousy day. Is that right?"

No one answered. Fran wouldn't have even considered answering, not in a million years.

Mr. Crowley's right eye twitched. The blue vein that ran down his forehead to his eye was pulsing. "You think I don't have anything better to do? Huh? Do you?" He jumped up. One quick long stride brought Crowley to Owen's desk. Owen began shifting uncomfortably in his seat as Crowley leaned over him. "Who said you could wear those glasses? Give them to me!"

"Uh, they're prescription," Owen mumbled, barely audible.

"They're *what?*"

"They're," Owen's voice cracked, "prescription."

Crowley stared down at the teenager in obvious disgust. "Take them off."

"Uh, okay, but I need them to—"

"This is detention, Lasker. You won't be doing any reading. Take them off."

Owen took the glasses off, blinking nervously. For years, kids had always picked on Owen, calling him "the mouse." Poor Owen, thought Fran. The truth was, there *was* something reddish about his eyes, like an animal caught in the glare of approaching headlights.

"You'll get them back after detention," Crowley said. "That is . . . if you ever make it out of here. What are you doing in detention, anyway? A smart kid like you."

"I don't know, sir."

Crowley's jaw clenched and unclenched. "You don't know?"

"Uh, Mr. Santana didn't like my term paper, for some reason. He wouldn't tell me why."

"He wouldn't, huh?"

"No, sir."

Crowley turned and headed back to his desk, muttering, "It was probably so pompous it made him sick."

"Maybe that's it," Owen agreed in his squeaky voice.

Crowley whirled and stared at Owen until he sunk another inch lower in his chair. The

DEADLY DETENTION

tension in the room was electric. For a moment, Fran wondered if Crowley was going to hit him.

The teacher began pacing the room slowly, like a caged tiger. "You kids are supposed to be the smart ones," he said, his voice filled with disgust. "The smartest of the smart. And look at you. Six of the smartest kids in the school! And what do you . . ?"

He broke off, turning angrily to the blackboard. He found a piece of yellow chalk in the grooved tray at the blackboard's base and wrote on the board, THE STUPID CLUB, in big block letters. He wrote so hard the chalk broke. With a second piece of chalk, he underlined the word stupid several times. Underneath that he wrote their names:

JILL BERMAN
GLEN DAVIS
OWEN LASKER
MIKE MORRICONE
JACLYN PEETERS
FRAN WEBER

He dropped the chalk back into the tray and looked out at the students with those vague, watery eyes of his.

Mr. Crowley wore his hair in a military style buzz-cut which exaggerated the largeness of his ears and the bulldog quality of his heavy features. The only soft thing about him were his eyes. The teacher's eyes were brown and light and watery like the tea-colored whiskey he was rumored to drink between classes. In fact, his eyes matched the color of whiskey so exactly it was as if he had filled his entire body with whiskey, right up to the eyeballs.

"Morricone," he grumbled.

"Yeah."

"Can't you go a day without getting detention?"

"I guess not."

Again the tension in the room seemed to crackle. Mr. Crowley tilted his head to the side, eyeing Mike like a hawk who was deciding whether or not to strike. "What was it this time?" he asked finally.

"My car wouldn't start, so I was late for school."

"Really? You got detention for being late? I thought you were always late, Morricone."

"Yeah, well this time I didn't get here until after third period."

"Uh huh." Crowley laughed, but not like he thought it was funny. "Well, if you think you were late getting here, just wait till you see how late you are getting home!"

For a moment, Crowley kept his eyes locked on Mike's. Then he shook his head and made a clucking noise with his tongue. "Morricone, Morricone, Morricone."

"What?"

"Math whiz, aren't you? Captain of the chess team, isn't that right?"

"Yeah. But what I really like is wrestling, you know, because—"

"Sure, sure. What's your grade-point average, Morricone?"

"Sir?"

"You heard me, what's your grade-point average?"

"Three point seven."

Tsk, tsk—the Corporal sucked on his tooth twice in a row. "Look at him, gentlemen. Our school's leading goof-off. Tries to act so cool. And he's pulling down a three point seven. Morricone, did it ever occur to you that if you were to do some serious studying, you could be number one in this school?"

Three years ago, thanks to Mr. Crowley, Harrison High had begun posting grade-point averages every month on the school bulletin boards, with the leaders announced over the P.A. system. At the end of the year, the highest average for each class won a prize. Each year, the competition had grown more and more fierce. As a result, grades had risen steadily, and this year the P.T.A. had given Mr. Crowley a prize of his own—for coming up with the idea of posting grades.

"I mean, why do you think Lasker won first place last year?" Crowley asked Mike. "Do you think it was by being a lazy good-for-nothing immature little clown such as yourself, Morricone? No! Owen hit the books every night like the genuine weenie that he is. Right, Lasker?"

"Right, sir."

"Right." Crowley headed back to his desk, then stopped, staring straight at Fran. He looked shocked. *You of all people,* he seemed to be saying. He shook his head in disgust. Once again, she lowered her eyes, looking down at her hands. They were trembling.

"Okay, kids," he said, "let's get to work."

He picked up his black briefcase and slammed it down hard on the metal desktop. Then he flicked open the metal latches with two rapid clicks, as if he were loading a rifle. The briefcase popped open. Crowley took out several tall blue cans of Comet cleanser which he slapped down onto the desk. Then he took out steel wool balls and sponges.

He scanned the room briefly. "Lasker," he said curtly.

"Yes, sir."

"Be a good little mouse and scurry down to the basement, would you? I want you to fetch me some buckets of warm, soapy water from the custodian."

"Yes, sir." Owen was blinking rapidly now, close to tears—he hated to be called "mouse."

"Now, Lasker."

Owen scurried out the door.

DEADLY DETENTION   43

Like everyone else, Fran was staring—transfixed by the cleaning materials on the teacher's desk. They looked like instruments of torture. What did Crowley have in mind? Was he going to scrub them to death?

The large man sat down on the edge of the metal desk. "Okay," he said. "Here's your detention assignment." He paused, the tension mounting. "Look around you."

Fran looked around. So did the other students. Which meant they were looking mainly at each other, sharing expressions of fear and disbelief.

Crowley said, "This room is school property, ladies and gentlemen. Lent to you for free. So what do you do with it? You wreck it, like you wreck everything else."

He sucked on a tooth. "So! Your job will be to remove every bit of graffiti from the desks. From the walls. From every part of this room. You will clean up every bit of dried chewing gum and crap that all the lousy students, such as yourselves, have stuck under there. You will scrub, and you will work, until this room is spotless and shiny and new and back to just the way it was when it was given to you." His voice rose in volume, as if it were getting away from him. "Do you UNDERSTAND?"

Fran's mouth was hanging open. Was he serious? But Crowley was acting so angry that no one risked a single groan of complaint. The teacher slammed the desk with his hand. "Do you understand?"

There was a mumbled "Yes, sir," from the entire group.

Crowley smiled slightly. "Good."

He picked up a ball of steel wool, tossed it up and down lightly in his large palm, then whipped it at Glen, saying, "Think fast, Davis."

Glen caught the steel wool ball with one hand.

Fran caught another ball of steel wool with two hands, but at least she caught it. Jill reached up for hers, missed it, and caught the ball in the face. Jaclyn giggled.

"Don't laugh," Crowley said. "It's hard to be coordinated when you're the size of a school bus."

"Hey," Fran said softly. "C'mon."

Crowley looked surprised. He walked over to Fran's desk. He stared down at her. She interlaced her fingers tightly, trying to stop their shaking. "You got a problem, Weber?"

Fran looked back up at the teacher. Trying to keep her face and her voice from trembling, she said quietly, "Her weight is none of your business."

The Corporal did a fake double-take. "None of my business? And who do you think you are, Weber? The school nurse?" He made his voice go sickeningly sweet, as if he were talking to a newborn baby. "In case you hadn't noticed, Fran, your pal Berman has a little bit of a weight problem. I'm trying to remind her of that fact because I am concerned about her health, understood?"

"It's okay, Frannie," Jill said quickly. "Don't worry about me."

Crowley spun around, staring at Jill. He draped a big smile across his sour features. "Now isn't that sweet," he said.

He walked among the desks, carrying the remaining balls of steel wool. He placed one on Mike's cap. He wiggled Jaclyn's in front of her until she snatched for it—several times—each time Crowley pulling the steel wool away at the last second. Finally, he dropped the steel wool into the lap of her crinkly vinyl skirt.

"I hope you're here for violating the Harrison High dress code," he told her dryly.

"There is no dress code," she said.

"Well, you're still violating it."

The door opened and Owen lumbered in, struggling under the weight of two yellow plastic buckets of sudsy water. He slopped some water on the floor.

"Lasker," Crowley said, "you klutz."

"Sorry."

Crowley checked his watch against the wall

clock. It was 4:15. "All right," he said. "Listen up."

As if they weren't listening already.

"I'll be back at exactly . . . 5:15." He pressed something on his watch, apparently setting a timer. "That gives you one hour to do your task. One hour, ladies and gentlemen." He crossed to the door.

He was halfway out the door when he turned back.

"Oh, and one more thing." His voice sounded like it had sand in it. "When I come back, the job had better be done."

Four

Owen was still standing next to the buckets of sudsy water. Everyone else was frozen in their seats. It was as if no one believed—or trusted—that Crowley had really left.

Then Jaclyn stood slowly, motioning the others for silence. She crossed to the door, where the paper towel dispenser hung. She pulled out several leaves of brown recycled paper, listening carefully the whole time. Then she opened the door a crack and peered out.

Then she stuck her whole head outside.

"He's really gone," she announced, as she closed the door again.

There was a collective groan, as if all the tension in the room were escaping at once.

"I don't believe this," Glen said.

Mike shook his head in amazement. "I have the worst luck. Fifty teachers, we have to draw the wacko." He was still smiling, but his eyes looked flat now, and angry.

"What's going on?" Owen asked. He started shifting his weight nervously from foot to foot.

"C'mon, tell me. I can't take it. What'd I miss?"

"We're supposed to clean up the whole room," Jaclyn explained.

"We have to remove every bit of graffiti," Jill said.

"And we can't go home until we're done," added Fran.

Owen's mouth dropped open. "Is he totally insane?"

"Yes," said Jaclyn. "He is."

"But that would take weeks," Owen whined. He started biting his nails and pacing at the same time.

"Months," corrected Glen. "I'm telling ya, the guy's a nutcase."

Fran stood. "Look," she said, "I'm sure the Corporal doesn't really expect us to clean it all up." She picked up a can of Comet. "We just have to be working hard whenever he checks in on us."

"Frannie's right," Mike said, standing as well. "C'mon. Let's get started."

Sighing dramatically, Jaclyn removed her orange cheerleading jacket, which she draped carefully over the back of her chair. Underneath she was wearing a tight, lacy white blouse. Her black walkman was strapped to her upper arm. She shook her mane of dirty-blond hair. "I'm not dressed for this," she complained.

"*I* am," Jill said. "That's the beauty of getting all your clothes at the Salvation Army. You're always prepared."

"Good." Jaclyn flashed a quick fake smile. "Then why don't you do all the cleaning for the rest of us?"

Fran was walking around the room now, sprinkling Comet on the desktops. She gave Jaclyn a look, considered saying something, but let it go.

"Hey," Glen said softly to Jaclyn. "He'll see it."

"See what?" Jaclyn demanded.

Glen nodded at the walkman. "Oh," Jaclyn said. "Yeah. Thanks." She angrily put her jacket back on, though she didn't zip it up.

Mike started distributing the sponges. "Let's get started, folks," he growled, in his best Crowley voice.

"Hey, you better eighty-six the joking around," Glen warned. "I'd like to get out of here sometime tonight."

"Yeah," Owen agreed. "And I want to live to be seventeen."

Jill wet a blue sponge in the sudsy water and wrung it out over her desk. Then she started scrubbing away. "You know, this is kind of fun, actually," she said. "Kind of like arts and crafts."

"Oh, right," snarled Jaclyn.

Glen took out a penknife. He unfolded the blade.

"Good thinking, Glen," Owen joked. "Let's stab him."

"Right," said Glen. He sighed. "Well, here goes." Easily flipping over his desk with one hand, he started prying off what seemed to be decades worth of dried gum.

"Oh, gross!" Owen said, when he looked under his own desk. "No way! I can't do this!"

"Try to think of it like we're archeologists," Fran told him.

"And what are we trying to find out?" Owen asked. "If kids chewed gum twenty years ago? I think I already know."

"This is so unfair," Jaclyn said, halfheartedly wiping her desktop with a moist sponge. "I'm going to have my mother complain to the principal about this. You watch. Crowley's going to be out of here by next Monday."

"I hope *we're* out of here by then," cracked Mike.

"There's nothing they can do about Crowley," Jill said. "For one thing, he's union. And anyway, the parents all worship him."

"They think we need a guy like that to whip us into shape," said Owen. "It's so ridiculous. I mean, I'd study hard no matter what."

"Well, you're a brown-noser," Jaclyn said.

Owen looked pained. "Oh, like I'm the only one in here trying for high grades?"

"Hey guys, listen to this." Fran was cleaning a section of the wall that had been particularly blessed with graffiti. "The Corporal's a psycho killer," she read. "Pass it on."

"Don't clean that one," Mike suggested. "It's too good."

"Here he comes!" Jill suddenly called.

Fran froze. She listened for the telltale sounds of footsteps approaching down the hallway.

Sure enough, the footsteps were only a few feet away.

Everyone started scrubbing furiously.

But the door to #301 didn't open. The footsteps went right by.

Fran breathed a sigh of relief. "Probably Mr. Binder," she whispered. Binder was the school's elderly, one-eyed custodian, as gray-faced as the cotton strands of his ancient mop. After hours, he roamed the halls like a ghost.

"Maybe it's Crowley," said Mike. "Checking up on us."

"He's probably pacing up and down the halls like a wild animal," Jaclyn said.

The six students listened a moment longer, but there was only the hissing of the pipes, the hum of the clock.

Jill giggled. "I was soooo scared," she said, flushing with excitement.

"Yeah," said Jaclyn flatly. "That was a real thrill."

Owen went back to cleaning, frantically scraping at his desktop with the steel wool. "Hey, Lasker," Mike said. "Pace yourself. We've got a whole hour."

"Yeah, thanks," Owen said. He gave Mike a bleary-eyed smile. But then he went back to scrubbing just as hard.

Like all rooms in Harrison High on even the coldest days of the year, Classroom #301 was hot. Fran wiped some sweat from her forehead with the back of her hand. "How are we supposed to clean the stuff that's been carved into the desks?" she wondered. "I mean, we'd need a sand blaster to do this job right."

"Maybe we should just blow up the whole school," Owen suggested. He howled.

"I am so *sick* of this place," said Glen, struggling to pry off a particularly stubborn piece of gum.

"Just a few more months and we're out of here," Jill told him.

"Don't rub it in, Berman," said Mike. "I've got another year of jail to go."

"Oh, right." Jill smiled apologetically. "Well, you're lucky, let me tell you. Applying to colleges is a major drag."

"Oh, come on, Berman," said Glen. "You're a brain. You'll get in anywhere you like." There was more than a hint of jealousy in his voice.

"Maybe so," said Jill. "But my parents are totally broke. If I don't get a full scholarship someplace, I'll have to go to a state school."

"What's the matter with that?" Mike asked. "Harrison High turned you off to public education?"

Jill bit her lip nervously. "I'm serious. You know, sometimes I wish I'd just gone to Blanchard like my sisters."

The Annette C. Blanchard School was one of the two other high schools in the area. Fran's cousin Ruthie went there. You didn't need good grades to get into Blanchard; not like at Harrison. Blanchard had no reputation for academic excellence. In fact, there was a reputation for academic lousiness.

"I know this guy at Valley," said Glen, naming the third local high school. "He's captain of the basketball team—Moorehouse? Anyway, he says in English they read like one book a year."

"Unbelievable," said Mike. "What a life."

"Yeah, but who wants to go to school with a bunch of retards?" asked Jaclyn.

Jill raised her hand. "I would. Then at least no one expects anything of you."

"It's true," agreed Fran. "I'm so tired of hearing how many Harrison kids have gotten into Ivy League schools."

"Those P.A. announcements are the worst," said Jaclyn.

Harrison's principal, Mr. Franklin, liked to interrupt the day with news bulletins about how well certain Harrison alumnae were doing. "Franklin always gets so choked up," Jaclyn said. "Everytime he gets to say the words Harvard, Princeton, or Yale, he starts crying."

"I'm sure you wouldn't mind if he was announcing your name," Owen said.

Jill covered her ears with her hands. "Okay, you know what? We've got to stop talking about this right now or I'm going to have a stroke."

"Oh, stop," Jaclyn said.

"Full scholarship," Jill reminded her. "You know how hard that is to get?"

"How about if you got like a partial scholarship?" Fran asked. "Couldn't your folks swing—"

"No. It has to be total. That's why I'm so stressed."

Jaclyn tossed her wet sponge down with a splat. Her blue eyes were gleaming with mischief. "Relax, Berman," she said. "I promise you, your worries are over."

Jill looked surprised. "Really? Gee, thanks. But what . . . ?"

DEADLY DETENTION 55

"*Allll* over."

Jill blinked. "What do you mean?"

"You can't get a scholarship."

"Why? Wh-what are you talking about?"

"Oh, you could have gotten one, sure. But not now, not after today."

"Oh, *right,*" Jill said, but she looked scared.

Jaclyn's pretty red lips curled into a tiny smile. "I'm not fooling, Jill. I'm serious."

Beads of sweat started popping out on Jill's upper lip. "Wh-what do you mean?"

"Detention, Jill. Think about it."

Everyone had stopped to watch now. Jaclyn's smile broadened. "Detention goes on your transcript. You think some school is going to pay for a delinquent's tuition? No way. When they see detention on your record, your scholarship is out the window."

"She's just teasing you," Fran assured Jill.

But Jill didn't take her eyes off Jaclyn. Her face had turned slightly gray. She stood up quickly, covering her mouth with her hand as if she might vomit.

"Hey," Mike said, moving toward the heavyset girl. "Don't even listen to her. You know Jaclyn. She's just trying to make you crazy."

"Sorry—I—it's—" Jill stammered. She clutched Mike's hand. "It's just—I sometimes get—these—anxiety attacks."

"Oh, great," Jaclyn said. "Welcome to Room #301, Harrison High's sanitarium."

"Jaclyn! Shut up!" snapped Fran. She moved quickly to Jill's side. "It's okay, Jill," she said. "There's nothing to be scared of."

But Jill was clutching her chest now, and her face was looking paler and grayer by the second. Fran could feel the panic rising in herself as well. "You want to sit down?" she asked quickly.

"Good idea, good idea," said Owen, clapping his hands. "C'mon, Jill, sit down."

"No, I'm okay," Jill said, leaning up against the wall. She didn't look okay. "Oh—oh—" she moaned.

"I'm going to get help," Fran said, starting for the door.

"No!" It was Jill. She had spoken sharply enough to stop Fran in her tracks. "It'll—pass," she said.

"She's right," Mike said. "Crowley's not going to be much help here."

Returning to Jill's side, Fran repeated firmly, "Jill, listen to me. There's nothing to be scared of." For lack of anything better to do, she kept saying these words.

"Oh, God! Oh, God!" Jill cried suddenly.

Fran and Mike both had a hold of her now.

"Breathe deep," Fran instructed.

Jill tried to breathe deep, but her breath came in short, stuttering gasps.

"Slow. Slow and deep. That's it," Mike said.

"And again," coached Fran.

"And again," repeated Mike.

Slowly the look of panic in Jill's round, doughy face began to fade.

"Feeling better?" Fran asked finally. Jill nodded. Fran sighed, the tension in her own body relaxing as well.

"Okay," Fran said to the rest of the group. "She's okay now."

The other kids all started talking at once. "Quiet," Mike warned.

Everyone was instantly quiet.

"Is he coming?" Owen asked, looking terrified

"No, but if we're too loud, he will," Mike said.

Jill had taken off her glasses and was rubbing her face with both hands. "Hey, Berman," Mike said with an easy grin. "That happen often?"

Jill nodded, her eyes lowered. "Actually, yes. I—I go to this shrink," she admitted. "He wants me to take Valium or something, but I keep hoping these attacks will just pass."

Jaclyn made a tiny circle around her ear with her forefinger—the international symbol for cuckoo.

"Jaclyn," Fran said in a warning voice. "Give her a break, would ya?"

There were tears in Jill's eyes now. Pushing past Mike and Fran, she tried to go back to cleaning her desk as if nothing had happened.

"Sorry about that, guys," she mumbled. "I'm fine now."

Mike and Fran exchanged glances. Mike shrugged.

"You want to talk about it?" Mike asked Jill.

Jill didn't look up from her scrubbing. "No. I don't want to talk about it. But thanks."

"Good," said Jaclyn. "Because I don't want to hear about it."

Fran shot Jaclyn a pleading glance. "C'mon," she told Jill. "It's better to talk about it. Besides, you're among friends."

"With one exception," Owen said, glaring at Jaclyn.

Jill wrung her sponge nervously with both hands, as if it were a security blanket. "It's just . . . I feel like I'm under so much pressure, you know? My family's . . . never had a straight-A student before."

"So be happy," Jaclyn said. "I mean, Glen's family has never had a straight-A student. And they never will."

"Thanks a lot," said Glen.

"I *am* happy," Jill said. "But it's just . . . my parents are soooo excited. It's like they won the lottery or something. They brag about me every day to every single person they meet. The dentist, the mailman—it's always, 'Have you met our daughter, the genius?' 'Did you know Jill is going to win the Nobel Prize some day?' And . . . and I get so scared about letting them

DEADLY DETENTION 59

down. And now I go and get detention. I just feel so . . ." All at once, the heavy girl was crying. "So . . . dumb!" she said as she finally managed to finish her sentence.

"You're not letting anyone down," Mike assured her.

"Jill, detention is completely no big deal," Fran said. "It doesn't mean anything. Jaclyn was just teasing."

Tears were streaming down Jill's round cheeks. She covered her face in her hands. "Oh, God, I'm so embarrassed."

"Don't be," Fran told her. "We all know what you're going through. Don't we, guys?"

"My mother can't sleep the night before I have a test," Owen said.

"You're lucky," Glen said. "With seven kids, my parents couldn't care less what I do. They don't even come to my games. And all I hear about all the time is how great my brothers did in school."

Fran gave him a sympathetic smile. Glen was the youngest in his family. He had four older brothers—all of whom had been great athletes and good students as well. As amazingly good-looking as he was, Glen really had it hard in his own way.

"I once brought home all A's," Mike said. "My dad said, 'You can do better.' Like he was so used to putting me down, he couldn't help himself. So I figured, to hell with it."

"What is this?" Jaclyn asked, as if talking to herself. "Group therapy?"

"Maybe it is," Fran said. "What's wrong with that?"

The cheerleader shrugged defiantly.

"Yeah. What about you?" Mike asked Jaclyn. "Don't you have anything you want to share with the class?"

"Not a thing."

"That's a laugh," Mike said. To the rest of the group, he said, "Jaclyn's mom pushes her so hard I'm surprised she doesn't come to school with her every single—"

"HEY!" Jaclyn almost shouted. Now she smiled. "Mike," she said sweetly. "You're cruisin' for a bruisin'."

Jill had stopped crying, but she was still sniffling loudly. "Here," Fran said, giving her a paper towel.

"Thank you." Jill blew her nose with so loud a honk that she laughed. Which made everyone laugh. "Wow," she said, "paper towels. So gentle on the nose." She blew her nose, another honk.

"You want a glass of water or something?" Glen asked her.

"No," Jill said. "But thanks." She thought a moment. "But I'll take an M&M." She fed herself several.

Fran wrapped her long, thin arm around Jill's shoulder. "You feeling better?"

DEADLY DETENTION 61

Jill nodded, chewing.

"Good," Mike said. He opened the door and stuck his head outside, glancing down the hallway. "Because I think we better get back to work or Crowley will—"

The strong, hairy hand closed around the back of Mike's neck.

"Or Crowley will what?" the teacher asked.

Five

"Will *what*, Morricone?" repeated Crowley, his grip tightening.

"Please—don't—" Mike said. He spun away. For a big strong guy, there was a surprising amount of fear in Mike's dark eyes.

A big grin spread slowly across Crowley's face. "What's the matter, Morricone? You look petrified. And I thought you were such a tough guy. Aren't you a tough guy, Morricone?"

"Sure," Mike said unsurely.

Crowley lowered his face right into Mike's. "Then how come you're so scared of me?"

He's like a dog, Fran thought, a dog who smells fear.

"Uh, the way you came up behind me," Mike stammered. He stepped back so quickly that he stumbled over a chair leg.

Crowley shook his head and chuckled. "What a sissy."

He started walking silently through the rows of desks, pausing to inspect the students' work.

"Not bad, people. Not bad at all. At this rate, you'll have this room cleaned up by tomorrow morning, just in time for first period class."

Fran kept her head down, eyes focused on her cleaning task.

"Maybe now you'll think twice before you write on your desks again, what do you say?"

Crowley slowly circled, letting each student feel his presence as he hovered behind them. When he passed Fran, she smelled the unmistakable perfume of liquor. There was no doubt about it. He'd been drinking.

Crowley crossed to the door. "Just remember, no one leaves this room until I get back. And no one's going home until this job is done. No one."

The door slammed shut.

The six students didn't move until the sound of Crowley's footsteps had faded far down the hallway. Even then, they didn't move. For several minutes, everyone kept working in a strained silence.

"The guy should be put away," Mike muttered.

"Shut up," said Glen.

More silence.

"So what about you, Fran?" Owen asked. He spoke in a low voice, almost a whisper, as if at any second Crowley might pop up from behind his desk. "What schools are you applying to?"

Fran nodded her head at Jill, trying to indicate to Owen to pick a different subject.

"Oh, you can talk about it," Jill said, catching the look. "I'm feeling all better now. I get like that but then it's gone, you know." She grinned. Behind her thick glasses, her eyes were still red.

Owen was waiting for an answer. "Oh, I'm trying a bunch of places," Fran said.

"All Ivy League," Jaclyn said, "I'm sure."

"Yeah," said Fran, "but my first choice—well, my dream, you know—is to go to Yale."

"So you're saying you want to go to the best school in the country?" asked Mike. "Weird."

Smiling, Fran said, "Yeah, my mom has always had this idea in her head, that that would be the greatest thing. You know . . . daughter of grocery store owner goes to Yale. I think I remember her telling me about Yale when I was still in the crib!"

"Get out," Jill said, with a laugh.

"I'm serious. She sang me boola-boola as a lullaby."

"You shouldn't go to some school just because your mom wants you to go there," Mike said.

"Oh, I know. I want to go there, too. For the drama. It's supposed to be incredible."

"Frannie Weber at Yale," Jill said, her eyes bright with admiration. "That would really be a pisser."

"Yeah. Well, don't worry, I'm sure I won't get in."

"You'll get in," Glen predicted.

Fran blushed. "Thanks."

"You'll *definitely* get in," Jill said.

"Well, I hope so," said Fran. She laughed. "My poor mom has even become religious lately. She's started praying that I'll get in!"

"You've got the grades, what are you worrying about?" Jaclyn asked.

"Well, it's not just grades for a place like that," Fran said. "Everyone who applies has good grades. So then it comes down to the extra things, like the interview, afterschool activities . . ."

"Like cheerleading," Jaclyn said, stretching athletically.

"Yeah," said Fran. "Me, I have just about zero afterschool activities."

"You've got the Lantern," Glen reminded her. The Lantern was the school yearbook.

"Yeah," Fran said. "And drama, and that's about it. Most kids have like these endless lists."

"Oh, well, who wants afterschool activities at a place like Harrison, anyway?" Mike said. "The only good afterschool activity is getting home."

"Which it looks like we're never going to do," Glen said.

There was another long lull in the conversation, everyone fidgeting, watching the clock, which showed ten after five. Then Owen said, "Doesn't *anyone* want to know where *I'm* applying?"

Fran smiled. "Sorry. Where?"

Owen leaped to his feet and lifted his short arms over his head, hands clasped in a gesture of triumph. "I'm not applying anywhere. I'm already in. Early Admission. MIT." He took a bow. "Thank you, thank you, one and all."

For a moment, there was a stunned silence in the room. Then Fran said, "Congratulations! That's excellent!"

"I know," Owen agreed proudly. He gave Jaclyn a smirk, made a gun with his finger and fired it at her.

"Gee, that's the perfect place for you, Lasker," Jaclyn said. "Egghead school."

"You wish you could go there," Owen said.

"Right," said Jaclyn. "I want to hang out with a bunch of geeky kids who can't see past their computer screens."

"That's right," Owen said. "Make fun. Let's see what you say when I make my first million."

"You can make all the money in the world," said Jaclyn. "You'll still be a geek."

Mike was staring straight at the cheerleader. "And where are you applying? Prison, I hope."

Jaclyn laughed hard, then stopped short. "That was so funny I forgot to keep laughing." She tossed aside her sponge. "Actually," she said, "my first choice is Penn, cause my sister Jess is there, and she says they've got these great sororities." She glanced sideways at Glen. "And this *incredible* social life."

Glen didn't seem to have heard. But Fran knew it was an act. Jaclyn was needling him, and he was feeling it. Poor Glen. Why did he take it? she wondered.

Jaclyn watched her boyfriend working on the underside of his desk with the knife. "What about you?" she asked. "You haven't told us *your* college plans, Glen."

Glen pried off a piece of gum that went flying into the radiator. "Well, my only A's are in math," he said glumly, "but I'm not too worried, you know. I think I've got a good shot at a basketball scholarship somewhere."

Jaclyn put her arm around the boy's broad shoulders. "Isn't it amazing how good Glen is in math, when he's so stupid in every other subject?"

Glen pulled his shoulder free.

"Aw," Jaclyn said, "look at him, he's sulking. Did I insult you? I said you were great in math. He is, too," she said, addressing the room in general. "I even think he's got a shot at winning the Walton."

Isaac Walton was this famous and popular math teacher who had taught at Harrison for years. When he died, he left money in a trust fund to pay for an annual math contest. Anyone in the school could take the test, which they gave right before Christmas break. In addition to prize money, the winner got a trophy (which was awarded at a special assembly), and *The Bergen Record* usually ran the winner's picture on their front page.

"Just think, Glen," Jaclyn said. "In a couple of weeks, you could win a whopping hundred dollars." To the rest of the group, she added, "So dorky."

"Well, it is prestigious, though," Jill said.

"Who asked you?" Jaclyn said with a fake smile.

"Look, Jaclyn," Fran said. "You're not with the cheerleading team right now, okay? You're with us. So how about we all just try to get along? I mean, we've got enough to worry about with Crowley on our hands."

"Oooh, I'm so sorry," Jaclyn said. "I forgot Frannie Weber was here, Miss Goody-goody."

Fran shrugged. "I'm serious."

"Whoop-de-doo." Jaclyn pulled on Glen's arm. "What's the matter?" she demanded.

He pulled his arm away. Then he stood.

Jaclyn watched him, her ice-blue eyes not blinking. "Where are you going?"

He didn't answer. She stood, fist on hip, as Glen walked right past her. He started cleaning another desk, one right next to Fran's. Frannie's heart rate doubled.

Jaclyn watched them a moment, her tongue pushing out her cheek, her eyes frigid with anger. "I don't know what you're trying to pull," she said tensely.

"I'm not trying to pull anything." Glen turned his new desk over and started working the gum with his knife. "I'm just doing what Crowley told us to do."

"Get back here," Jaclyn said.

Glen didn't respond.

"Now!"

Glen kept working, his head down.

Jaclyn chuckled. "Fine. You're dead meat, Davis. You hear me? Dead. Meat."

Glen lifted his head from his work and gave her a sad look. Then he went back to cleaning.

Fran was having trouble concentrating. Was it her imagination? Or was Glen gradually moving his desk even closer as he cleaned?

He caught her eye. His brown doe-eyes gleamed. He smiled easily. "So?" he said softly, "You come here often?"

Fran laughed and blushed.

Fran was a popular girl, but she had never been this close to Glen Davis before. And Glen close-up was even more impressive than Glen from a distance.

He was wearing a brown fur-lined corduroy jacket, which he wore open over a black T-shirt, and a pair of faded light-blue dungarees, all purchased at the GAP. In fact, with his cleft chin and heart-shaped face, the teenager could easily have passed for one of those GAP models featured in the ads in the bus kiosks around Harrison and other northern New Jersey towns. He was *that* good-looking. And that soft voice and gentle manner of his—they were real killers.

In her embarrassment, Fran returned to scrubbing, working twice as hard as before.

"You look like you know what you're doing," Glen told her, as he watched her clean.

"What? Oh!" She laughed. "I guess I do. My parents, you know, well, they give me plenty of chores." Even without looking, she could feel Jaclyn's eyes boring down on her and Glen. She kept her head down.

"You're an only child, right?" Glen asked.

"Yup. It's just me." The way he was talking—so softly—and the way he was staring at her with those soft brown eyes, it was as if they were the only two in the room. Fran felt the tips of her ears turn hot and red. She worried they might be glowing.

"Oh, by the way." Glen cuffed his forehead as if annoyed at himself for forgetting. "I've been meaning to tell you. You were really great in that play. What was it?"

"You Can't Take it With You?"

Glen grinned. It was a sexy grin—warm and winning. "Yeah, yeah, that's the one."

Fran's blush deepened. "Glen, that was last fall."

"Was it? Oh, yeah. Well, I've been meaning to tell you."

"I'll flay you alive," said Jaclyn, without looking up from the desk she was cleaning.

Glen gave Fran a look as if to say, Don't mind her. But there was fear in his eyes.

Owen wrung out his sponge in the bucket and said, "Only two more minutes, guys."

Mike glanced at the wall clock. Owen was right. It was thirteen after five.

"Thank goodness!" Jill crumpled her bag of M&Ms. "I don't think I can last much longer." She laughed. "I'm out of food."

Outside the windows, the sun was setting. Dusk made the room—and detention—seem even grimmer.

Owen stretched. "Sayonara, Harrison," he called. "Bye-bye, Mr.—"

The door flew open. Crowley rushed into the room and straight to where Owen was sitting. He grabbed Owen's desk, yanking it away from the skinny boy.

And then Crowley lifted the desk up in the air, right over Owen's head.

Six

"No!" gasped Owen, covering his head with his hands. "My God! Please!"

Mr. Crowley looked down at Owen, as if surprised. Then he laughed. "You thought I was going to hit you?" He laughed harder. "You fool, Lasker. You think I would do something that stupid? Is my name up there?" He nodded behind him, to where, on the blackboard, the Stupid Club names were listed. "I just wanted to see if you had done your job. See if there was any graffiti left on this desk."

Crowley studied the desktop closely, holding it right up to his face. His jaw clenched. He lowered the desk to the floor slowly. "What have you been doing?" he asked quietly.

"Cleaning," said Owen.

"You've been slacking off, haven't you? Just sitting around, shooting the breeze!"

Owen said, "No, sir, we—"

"Shut up!"

Owen shut up. Crowley grabbed him by the

shoulder. He pulled him toward the desktop. "What's this?"

"A-a-a desk."

He yanked him closer. "No, fool. What's *on* the desk?"

"There's . . . some . . . graffiti. But sir? We've been trying to clean it, it's just that—"

"I said SHUT UP!"

Owen gasped in fear. Crowley let him go. He crossed to his own desk. He was a little unsteady on his feet, Fran noticed. He wiped some spittle from his mouth.

"I just don't understand you guys. I give you a simple task and you don't do it. I mean, don't push your luck, you know what I mean? You've already got detention. What do you want me to do, keep you here all night?" It was one of Crowley's favorite threats. "I'll do it, too. You know I will. Since you seem to want to stay after school so badly, I'll lock you all up so you can spend the night right here."

Despite the steam heat hissing into the room, Fran felt a chill race down her spine.

Crowley kept rubbing his nose and making that tsk sound. "Weber!" he barked.

Fran's heart jumped. "Yes?"

"Get up here." She walked up to where he was standing, trying to keep her bare knees from knocking.

Crowley looked at her for a moment. Then he turned and pointed. "Peeters!"

Jaclyn appeared totally calm. Even if it was an act, it was impressive, Fran thought. "What?" Jaclyn asked coldly.

"Get up here."

Jaclyn looked unruffled, but she did as she was told.

"Okay," Crowley told the two teenagers. "I want you two to tell me honestly. Is there any graffiti left in this room?"

"Yes," Jaclyn began, "but—"

"No BUTS!" Crowley cut her off. "You heard her," he told the other students. "She said yes. Your own classmate admits that you blew your assignment. What about you, Weber? Is there any graffiti left in this room? Of course there is. Okay. You and Peeters. Go to Binder and get us some fresh water. Now!"

Fran and Jaclyn both stood there, gaping. "But . . . but what do we need fresh water for?" Fran asked, and her voice betrayed her—it shook.

Crowley growled, "You're supposed to be such a smart student, aren't you, Weber? Maybe you can figure it out."

"But," Fran continued, as gently as she could, "there's no way we can ever—"

"Weber!" Crowley cut her off again.

"Yes?"

"Go."

Fran and Jaclyn exchanged glances. Then they both started for the door. Owen piped up from the front row, "But detention is over, sir. It's 5:21."

Pivoting sharply, Crowley swung his powerful arm right in Owen's face. Owen screamed. So did Fran.

Crowley stopped his fist inches from Owen's bulbous nose. He was showing the boy his watch. "What is that, Lasker?"

"A w-w-watch?"

"Right. I own a watch. I can tell time. Got it?"

Crowley turned back to Fran and Jaclyn. "Go," he ordered them again.

They went.

All the time that Fran and Jaclyn were gone, Crowley sat on the edge of his desk, watching the other students. No one said a word. When Fran and Jaclyn finally returned with the buckets of fresh water, Crowley stood. "What took you so long?" he snarled.

"We couldn't find Mr. Binder," Jaclyn said. "We had to look everywhere."

"I think he went home," Fran said softly.

Crowley clenched and unclenched his jaw. "You need the custodian to fill up a bucket?"

It was Mr. Crowley who had told them to find Binder, thought Fran. She considered reminding Crowley of this fact. She considered it for only a moment. She remained silent.

"Okay," Crowley said. He pressed a button on his watch. "I'm going to give you all one more hour."

This time there were moans and groans. "You can't keep us here," Jaclyn began. "You're only allowed to keep us until—"

Crowley's bulldog look of fury was scary enough to silence even Jaclyn Peeters. "One last time," he said quietly. "You're going to stay until the job is done. Got it?"

He waited, letting his words sink in.

"I'll be back at 6:15. No one is to leave this room," he said. "On pain of death."

He crossed to the door. Before he left, and right before he closed the door hard, he added, "That's 6:15 *sharp*, ladies and gentlemen."

But 6:15 came. And went.

So did 6:30.

And still Mr. Crowley had not returned.

Seven

"This is insane," Mike said.

"He can't do this," Fran said. She tried to smile. "Can he?"

"I'm definitely getting him fired," Jaclyn vowed.

"I've got to get home for dinner," Glen said.

"Oh, please don't mention food," said Jill. The heavy girl clutched her stomach. "My stomach is rumbling like crazy."

"I've got such a headache," whined Owen, "you would not believe it." He started cracking his knuckles, one by one.

Mike said, "Maybe Crowley went home. Maybe he expects us all to leave."

"That doesn't sound like Crowley," said Fran.

"Yes it does," said Glen. "Then he can give us detention all over again."

For a moment, Fran and the other students sat in edgy and somber silence. No one was doing any cleaning, that was for sure. But everyone was still holding their paper towels and steel wool and sponges, ready to start cleaning the moment the door opened.

Fran watched the clock.

Six-forty.

"Maybe we should go look for him," Glen suggested.

"Go right ahead," Jaclyn said.

"I said we," Glen said.

Nobody moved.

"I've got a good idea," Jaclyn said. "Owen will go." She smiled sweetly. "Won't you, little mousie?"

"Don't call me that!" Owen cried.

"Jaclyn," Fran said with a sigh, "really."

"Really what?"

"I'll go," Jill offered.

"Oh, listen to her," Jaclyn said. "An hour ago, she was shaking like a lunatic. Now she's Miss Hero."

"Oh, well, I can explain that," Jill said. "See, I'm really pretty good in a crisis. It's only when I have too much time to think that—"

"No one's interested, Berman," Jaclyn said.

"Crowley's probably right outside in the hall," Mike said, lowering his voice. "Just waiting for one of us to open the door."

The thought was enough to shut everyone up again. The students waited. Fran could feel the tension and frustration mounting inside the room. She felt as if it would soon be hard for her to breathe.

"I'm going," she said, standing.

"Going where?" Owen squeaked. "Home?"

"No. To look for him."

Mike stood as well. "I'll go with you." Then Glen stood. Then Jill. Then Owen.

Standing last, Jaclyn said drily, "Looks like we're all going."

Fran was already at the door. She put her hand on the doorknob.

"What if he locked us in?" Owen asked in a whisper.

Fran turned the doorknob. The door was open.

"Thank God," Owen said.

"Lasker, get a life," Jaclyn said.

Outside Classroom #301, the hallway was dark. The hallways of Harrison were never much to look at, even during the day. Just a bunch of gray lockers and cinderblock walls that were glopped with yellowish paint. But now the overhead lights were off, so the hallway was lit only by tiny yellow safety lights, like the lights they turned on in movie theater aisles after the movie had started. Darkness made the hallway look downright sinister.

"Mr. Crowley?" Fran called.

No response.

"Mr. Crowley?" Jill asked in a whisper. She started opening locker doors.

Jaclyn pushed past the heavy girl. "Are you insane, Berman? You think he's hiding in one of the lockers?"

"I think he really forgot about us," Mike said. He twisted his white cap so that the brim faced front, then twisted it back again. "Unbelievable. What a jerk."

The six teenagers all stood in a little group outside of #301, as if afraid to go any further.

"Mr. Crowley?" Owen called loudly. "We're done with our assignment!"

Still no answer.

Jaclyn giggled.

"Where would he be?" Fran wondered.

"Teachers' lounge?" Jill guessed.

"The neighborhood bar?" guessed Mike.

"Sssh!" hissed Jaclyn, but she giggled some more. She playfully slapped Mike's arm. "You're terrible."

Fran glanced at Glen. Even in the darkness of the hallway, she could see the jealousy in his eyes. It was clear to Fran what Jaclyn was up to. Glen had flirted with her; now Jaclyn was taking her revenge.

"C'mon," Fran said, starting down the dark hallway. "Maybe we can find Mr. Binder or a teacher and tell them what happened."

But every classroom on the floor was dark.

The six students huddled by the door to the stairwell.

"I really don't think we should leave the floor," Owen said.

"Oh, grow up, Lasker," said Jaclyn, yanking open the stair door. "He's gone. Can't you get that through your head?"

She started down the stairs. Everyone followed.

The second floor hallway looked exactly like the first—dark, deserted, and dead. The teachers' lounge was at the other end of the hall. No light spilled out under the edge of the lounge door.

"I'm starting to get scared," Jill whispered, as they headed down the hall toward the closed door.

"I thought you were so good in a crisis," Jaclyn said.

"Hello?" Mike called loudly.

"Ssshhh!" Jaclyn told him, giving him another playful slap.

They reached the end of the hall. Fran knocked on the door.

Silence.

"Maybe he passed out," Jill said in the tiniest of whispers.

Jaclyn drew her finger across her throat and mouthed the word "Quiet!"

"Try again," Mike said to Fran.

Fran knocked louder.

Then Glen stepped forward and slapped the door with his open palm. He pounded. "Mr. Crowley?"

"He's not in there, brainiac," Jaclyn told him.

Glen glared at her. Then he tried the doorknob. He opened the door slowly, as if expecting Crowley to spring out at them with an ax. He reached his hand around inside the dark room, felt for the switch, and flicked on the lights.

Jill gasped.

Which made Fran gasp.

Then they laughed. Because the teachers' lounge was empty and ordinary looking. Three wooden desks, set up against the windows. An old beat-up sofa. A coffee machine. Dirty ashtrays. The leftover nasty smell of years of cigarette smoke had worked its way into the upholstery.

The students all crowded into the room, ogling the walls and furniture as if they believed Crowley might be hiding in here somewhere. "The bastard really went home," Mike said.

"Look at this," Glen said. He was pointing into one of the trash baskets. Nestled amid the cigarette butts, the Styrofoam coffee cups, and the crumpled phone message slips was an empty quart bottle of Jim Beam whiskey.

DEADLY DETENTION

"Wow. He isn't even trying to hide it," Fran said.

"That's a bad sign," said Jill.

The door swung shut behind them.

"Oh, my God!" Owen said.

His hand flew to his mouth.

He pointed.

Fran turned. On the back of the door was Mr. Crowley's dartboard. Six darts were clustered together in the bull's-eye, each dart skewering a small black and white photo. Something about the photos looked familiar. Fran stepped closer.

And now she saw what had made Owen gasp.

Crowley had cut out photos of all six kids in that room.

Eight

"It's our pictures," Owen cried, peering at the dartboard.

"No way," Mike said.

"Way," said Glen, stepping closer.

"What a sicko!" Jill said in a hushed whisper.

"Takes one to know one," Jaclyn said mildly. She pulled out the darts, stuffed the six pictures into the tight pocket of her short vinyl skirt, then stuck the darts back in the bull's-eye. "Now I *know* I can get him fired."

"Let's get out of here," Fran said.

No one required any further encouragement. The group hurried out the door, and down the stairs to the first floor. Mike was the first to reach the exit door at the end of the hall. He yelled, "Hasta la vista, Mr. Crowley, wherever you are!" Then he lowered his broad shoulder and hit the door hard.

It was the way cool kids left school each day, banging out, escaping to freedom like inmates breaking out of jail.

Only this time the door didn't budge.

Mike rubbed his shoulder where he had banged it. Then he grabbed the door's silver release bar with both hands and rattled it with all his might.

The door still didn't open.

When Mike turned back to the rest of the group, his jaw had dropped. "It's locked," he said.

"Uh oh," Owen said. He gulped.

"This way," Glen said quickly. He jogged down the hallway to the other exit door. Everyone trotted after him. But they stopped when they heard him rattling the door's release bar. The rattling told them the news before Glen did. "This one's locked, too," he called back. His voice echoed down the deserted hall.

"This is getting too weird," Jill said in a hollow voice. "Way too weird."

"Crowley must still be in here somewhere," Fran said, shivering. "That's all."

"Of course he's here," Jaclyn said. "There's no way he would just leave us locked up."

"You just said he was gone for sure," Glen reminded her.

"Well if we're locked in, then he's not gone," Jaclyn said. "Got it?"

"This way," Mike said, heading down the hall that led to the cafeteria.

Harrison High had two wings of classrooms. Where the two wings met there was a large, one-level square building. Here were the cafeteria, library, club and administration offices, all connected by a maze of hallways. In back of this central building there was a glass walkway that led to a separate round building—the gym.

The students did a full lap around the school's central square. They passed plenty of exit doors. But every door they came to was locked.

Fran struggled to keep calm. "Okay," she said, as they started down yet another hallway.

"What's okay?" Owen asked. "Nothing's okay. Why are you saying okay?"

"We're *going* to be okay," Fran said.

"MR. CROWLEY!" Glen shouted, cupping his hands to his mouth.

No response.

They entered the first floor hallway of the second wing of classrooms. On the wall was an endless bulletin board display of artwork done by freshmen—snowflakes depicted in every medium, from pen and ink to watercolors to oils. Fran had a memory flash. She had gotten an A on that same project her freshman year, photographing real snowflakes under a microscope. "No Two Alike," she had titled it. Her mom had kept the pictures on the fridge door all year. She was smiling as Jaclyn reached out a hand and ripped down several of the pictures. Jaclyn threw them up in the air and let them flutter back down in a brief snowfall.

"What are you doing?" Fran demanded.

"It wasn't me," Jaclyn said with a grin, her white teeth shiny in the dark.

"Some kids spent a lot of time on those pictures," Fran said.

"Oh, you're pathetic," Jaclyn told her.

"Jaclyn, c'mon," Glen said. "Fran's right. We can't break stuff."

"Why not?"

" 'Cause they'll know it was one of us," Glen reasoned.

Jaclyn's eyes were glittering. "How?"

"How?" Glen asked. "Who else would it be, Jaclyn? I mean, it sure looks like we're the only ones in the school."

"There's got to be some benefit to being locked in this lousy place," the cheerleader grumbled. She ripped down several more pictures, ripping them slowly in half.

Fran shook her head. She started walking on down the hallway. Everyone followed.

"We're not going to have to spend the night in here, are we?" Jill asked. "I don't think I could handle that."

"Me neither," agreed Owen. He was snapping his fingers now. The poor guy couldn't stay still for a second, thought Fran.

"We'll get out," Glen promised.

"My hero," Jaclyn said.

"We're not going to have to spend the night in here, are we?" Jill asked again.

"You just asked that," Owen reminded her.

"I know, but I couldn't help noticing that we're still locked in."

"I hope we do have to spend the night," Mike said. "That's probably the only way I'll be on time for school."

"We could make it like a pajama party," said Fran.

"No offense," Jaclyn said. "But if I was going to have a sleepover, it wouldn't be with you guys."

They had reached the exit door at the end of the hallway; this time it was Fran who tried the release bar. She rattled it desperately. Then she turned back and looked at the others. She shook her head.

"Oh, God," Jill said.

"Don't worry," Mike said. "We'll get out. Even if we have to break out." He took a running start and chinned himself up onto a window ledge. Then he unlocked the large window and raised the sash.

Icy air blasted into the hallway, instantly goosebumping the skin on Fran's bare arms.

"Great," Mike said, studying the window.

"What's wrong now?" Owen asked.

Mike jumped down, dusting off his hands.

"The wire mesh. To protect the windows? It's reinforced with iron bars. There's no way we can get out that way."

Owen moaned. He started pacing up and down and gesticulating wildly. "I don't believe this. This is absurd! I mean, how could Crowley do this to us? You know what I'm going to do? I'm going to sue! That's what I'm going to do! I'm going to sue him for every penny he's got."

"He probably doesn't have very many pennies," said Fran, "on a teacher's pay."

"We need a plan," said Glen.

"Right," said Jaclyn. "And who's going to think of one. You?"

"Sure," he said.

"Go ahead. Let's see you think your way out of this."

Glen thought. "I guess we have to sleep here," he said finally.

"Oh, great plan," Jaclyn said, patting his head. She gave him a small smile. "Stick to math."

"I've *got* to get home," Jill said. "I've got a lot of studying to do."

"Relax, dweeb," said Jaclyn. "You've got all your books, don't you? You can study right here, in the library."

"Oh, that really relaxes me," said Jill.

"Did I mention that I've got a chem final tomorrow?" Owen asked, still pacing.

"You've mentioned it several times," Jaclyn said.

"This is so unfair!" he whined. "I'm going to flunk. I'm serious! I'm going to flunk."

"Oh, do I hate that," Jaclyn said. "Did you ever notice, it's always the best students who worry the most before the tests?"

"What are *you* complaining about?" Mike asked her. "You always get A's."

"Yeah, but I don't sit around the night before pulling my hair out. I know I'm going to ace it. And that's that."

"Well you should start worrying," Jill said, "because we're locked in." She wrapped her pudgy arms around her large middle. Then she slid down the wall and sat on the hallway floor. "Am I the only one here with claustrophobia?"

"Where are you going?" Glen asked Jaclyn as she took off down the hall.

The cheerleader didn't answer, just kept marching down the hall. "I just figured out how to get us all out of here." She walked over to the water fountain, tucked her hair behind her ear, and slurped noisily.

"Oh, that's a big help," Mike said.

Jaclyn gave him a little grin. Then she wiped her mouth with the back of her hand. She turned and kept walking. She stopped at the square red box mounted at eye-level on the wall.

DEADLY DETENTION

She put her hand on the fire alarm's little lever.

"No!" Owen cried. "Are you crazy?"

"What's the matter?" Jaclyn asked.

"You can't pull the alarm. The police will come. We'll all get in trouble."

Jaclyn smiled. "Exactly. Listen to what you're saying. The police will come. They'll let us out. Get it?"

"Pull it!" Jill suddenly cried.

Jaclyn pulled the metal lever down, hard.

Nothing happened.

No alarm bells jangled through the halls. No sirens sounded in the distance. Nothing.

"That's strange," Glen said.

"Maybe it's ringing at the fire station," Fran said hopefully.

"I don't know," Mike said, taking off his cap and scratching his dark curly locks. "It always blasts out pretty loud during fire drills."

"You don't think that—?" Owen began. Then he went back to pacing.

"Don't think what?" Jill demanded.

"Nothing . . . nothing."

"What?"

Owen stopped again, his fingers fluttering nervously against his chin. "No, I was just thinking, if Crowley has really snapped, you know, and he's really locked us in here? Well . . . what if—" He broke off again.

Now everyone said, *"What if what?"*

"What if he turned off the alarm?" Owen finished. His eyes bulged. Apparently, his own reasoning had terrified him.

"Could he do that?" Fran asked. Tiny hairs were standing up on the back of her neck.

Owen was waggling all ten fingers in the air, hard, as if he were trying to air-dry his hands. It was one of the many manic mannerisms kids always teased him for. "Could he do that?" he cried. "It'd be a snap. All the wiring for the alarms and the phones and everything in this school goes through that big central control panel over by the library. Couple of snips with a scissors and presto! We're cut off."

Jaclyn started chewing a new piece of gum. "Lasker, you're clueless, you know that?"

Owen stopped shaking his hands. "How do you mean?"

"You think Crowley would mess up school property?"

Owen thought for a moment, then said, "If he's gone crazy, he's gone crazy." He went back to pacing again.

"That's crap," Jaclyn said. "He's probably walking around the school looking for us and we just missed him. C'mon, Glen."

She started walking down the hall, swinging

DEADLY DETENTION 93

her arms in that bouncy step of hers. For a moment, Glen didn't move.

Jaclyn glanced back over her shoulder. "I said come on."

"You want me to come with you?"

She walked on. "You got it, genius."

Glen shrugged. Stating the obvious, he explained to the others, "We're going to go check around." He sauntered off after Jaclyn.

Fran watched him go. With his broad shoulders and narrow hips, he had the natural gait of a true athlete. You could see how he might snake through the line as a tailback in football; you could see how this past season he had set a Harrison rushing record. In her heart, Fran knew he had only flirted with her to get back at Jaclyn; still, she was sorry to see him go.

"My mom is going to die," Owen whined. "She is going to die of worry. If I don't call in every five minutes, she has a heart attack."

"Call in?" Fran stared at Owen blankly for a second. "The phone!" she cried. Then she started running down the hall.

There was a pay phone outside the principal's office. Fran picked up the black plastic receiver just as Owen, Mike, and Jill rounded the corner. They all gathered around her.

"Well? Why aren't you calling?" Owen asked her nervously.

"Call the cops," Mike told her.

"Dial 911!" Jill said. "Dial 911!"

Fran held up the receiver, as if to show them her answer. "The line's dead," she said.

Nine

Jill's tiny hands flew up to the sides of her large head. "Oh, no," she gasped. "Crowley cut the line!"

She looked at Owen. Owen looked at Jill. Then they grabbed each other and started jumping up and down, chanting, "Crowley cut the line! Crowley cut the line!"

Fran was yelling, too. But then—

"Whoa! Hold it!" Mike reached out a powerful arm and grabbed Jill and Owen. He put another arm on Fran's shoulder, silencing her, calming her. "Guys," he said. "You're losin' it. This pay phone has been broken for weeks, remember?"

Fran, Jill, and Owen all stared at each other. Then they burst out laughing.

"Oh, God," Fran said.

"Mike's right," Jill said. "We *are* losing it."

"I've already lost it," mumbled Owen.

"I'm telling you, Crowley went home," said Mike. "Here." He opened the door to the principal's office. "We'll call from in here."

He turned on the lights.

The outer office belonged to the principal's secretary, old wrinkled Mrs. Merriwether. There were two green vinyl sofas catercornered against the walls. If you were sent to the principal, this is where you had to wait. On either side of the sofas were fake potted palms. Then there was a long row of gray filing cabinets. And then there was Mrs. Merriwether's desk, with its tiny cactus plant, framed photos of her grandchildren, and a little pink teddy bear whose T-shirt said, "I want to give you a hug!"

"Wow," Jill said, looking around the room.

"Wow what?" Mike asked.

"We're in the principal's office," she said.

"So?" asked Owen. "You've never been in here before?"

Jill was moving toward the wall of filing cabinets. "They've got our transcripts and personal files in here."

"Don't touch that!" Owen shrieked. "Are you bonkers, Berman? We'll all get expelled!"

Jill pulled her hands away from the filing cabinets as if she'd received an electric shock. "Good point," she said.

"What do you want to see your file for, anyway?" Mike asked her. "All it says is what a great student you are. If you want to read something interesting, take a look at *my* file. It probably takes up one whole drawer."

"We're not looking at *any* files," Owen insisted.

Mike strode to the secretary's large desk and plopped down in her black leather desk chair, swiveling around wildly. "Wheeeee!" He kicked his feet in the air like a little boy. "Funnnn!!!"

"C'mon, Mike," Fran urged him. "Call."

Mike picked up the phone. "Hello, Harrison High," he said in a pinched, nasal voice. "Miss Merriwether, Mr. Franklin's personal secretary, speaking. Can I help you? I'm sorry, but the principal is on another call at the moment. Can I give him a message?"

Owen whooped. "That's perfect," he said, giggling. "That's perfect!"

"You're looking for Mike Morricone?" Mike continued. "He's in detention, I'm sure. How do I know? Oh, well, Mike's *always* in detention. Whenever I want to find Mike that's the first place I—Oh, *Mr. Morricone*, how are you!"

Mike was doing a great imitation of Miss Merriwether's nervous gestures. Now his large hands fluttered around his hair as if rearranging it. "It's lovely to hear your voice, Mr. Morricone!"

Fran and Jill joined in the laughter.

"I see. You want to find Mike so you can beat up on him some more?"

Fran stopped laughing. So did Jill. Only Owen couldn't seem to contain himself.

"But you beat up on him almost every night, don't you, Mr. Morricone? Isn't that enough? I see. You want to start beating up on him during the school day as well. Well, I'm sure that's something we could handle for you. Oh, now, don't thank me, Mr. Morricone. We pride ourselves on being substitute parents. In fact, we have one teacher who would love to do this job for you. Mr. Crowley. The biology teacher, right. Yes, I'll get him right on it. Yes, Mr. Morricone."

Still pretending to be the secretary, Mike whispered several more soft "Good-byes" before he put the receiver back in its cradle.

"Is that true?" Fran asked softly. "About your dad?"

"Is what true?" Owen asked.

For a brilliant kid, he could be awfully dense sometimes, Fran thought.

"Nah," said Mike with a smile. He swiveled away in the chair, swiveled back. He was avoiding her eyes.

"Then why did you say it if it wasn't true?" Jill asked, looking concerned.

Mike had come to school on more than one occasion with bruises and black and blue marks. But he was a wrestler, Fran had always told herself. And he was a tough kid. It had never crossed her mind. "It *is* true, isn't it?" she asked again.

Mike flashed his standard crinkle-eyed grin. "Maybe it is, maybe it isn't."

"That means it's true," said Fran.

"I'm—I'm sorry, Mike," Jill said. "And I thought *I* had it bad."

Mike shrugged. "You do." He bit his lip and stared out the window. "It's not my dad's fault," he said. He grinned. "There's a recession out there, guys. He's been out of work all year. He's got to take it out on somebody."

Fran didn't return Mike's smile. "You should get help."

Mike laughed, as if this were a funny joke. "From who?"

"The police," said Jill.

"Wait a minute," Owen said. "You mean that was true? About your dad? Get a lawyer!" he said earnestly. "Hey, I've got two—no *three* uncles who'd be glad to help you out on a—"

"Forget it," Mike said. "If I ever made any kind of a fuss he'd kill me. Anyway, it's not so terrible. Least this way I don't have to worry about disappointing my old man the way the rest of you do. I know he's *always* disappointed."

Owen let out a whoosh of breath. "Wow. I don't know what I'd do if. . . . I mean, my parents, the worst they ever do is wring their hands. They would never . . . I guess I would just kill myself," he concluded.

"Oh, that's very helpful, Owen," Jill said.

"What? Oh, God," Owen said, his voice rising. "I wasn't suggesting that Mike—"

"Forget it," Mike said. He picked up the receiver again. "Let's get out of this dump."

"Please hurry," said Jill. "Being here after dark like this is really giving me the creeps."

"I guess I'll start with the police," Mike said. He placed one stubby finger in the 9 of the black phone's old-fashioned rotary dialer.

But he didn't dial.

When he looked up at the other students, his face was grave.

"It's locked," he said.

"What do you mean locked?" Owen asked.

"Locked, as in shut, as in they put this little lock on the phone so no students can make calls when they're not looking."

"Locked," Owen repeated numbly. Then he shouted out in frustration and fear.

Jill raced into the principal's inner office. "This one's locked, too," she called back.

"Okay, okay," Fran said. "Nobody panic." She started for the door. "I'm sure we can find a phone that's not locked."

"There's a phone in the library," Owen said, running past her and out into the hall.

"What about the homeroom phones?" Jill

asked. "Can they make outside calls or can they just call other classrooms?"

"Check!" Fran said. She watched as Jill jogged off down the hall. "I'm going to try the phone in the teachers' lounge," she told Mike.

"Good idea," Mike said.

Fran smiled shyly. "You're not really worried, are you?"

"Are you kidding? This is a blast. Anyway, it beats being home by a long shot."

Fran stood awkwardly in the doorway, her left hand holding her right elbow behind her back. She smiled sadly. "Yeah, I guess it does." She couldn't think of anything else to say. What could you tell a guy whose father beat him? "Well," she said, "I'll be right back."

"Okay."

Fran stuck her head back in the doorway almost at once.

"That was quick," Mike joked.

"Oh, where are *you* going to check?" she asked.

"Mr. Binder's got a phone in the basement, I guess I'll go down there."

Fran nodded. "Great. Hey, maybe Mr. Binder's still down there."

"At this hour?"

"Yeah. I guess you're right." She waved and disappeared again.

Mike waited until he was sure she was gone.

And even then, he stayed where he was, sitting behind the secretary's desk.

Ten minutes later, Fran was making her way back from the teachers' lounge. Like Miss Merriwether's phone, the teachers' lounge phone was also locked. She was halfway down the first-floor hallway when she heard the footsteps.

She turned sharply.

There was nothing in the hall, nothing but lockers, all of them shut.

"Mike?" she called.

Silence.

"Owen? Jill?"

Feeling foolish, she turned and continued walking.

But now she was sure of it, sure she was not alone. She stopped, listening hard. She heard a door scrape on its hinges.

"Jaclyn?" she called. "Glen?"

Her heart was pounding. Look at me, she thought. Scared silly. And of what?

She turned around again. Keeping her eyes on the long dark hallway, she started walking backward.

No one jumped out at her from the dark classroom doorways.

No demons popped out of the lockers to grab her in their claws.

DEADLY DETENTION

C'mon, she told herself as she reached the end of the hall. Get a grip, Weber!

She was still walking backward when she felt the body smack into her, the arms close around her.

She screamed.

Ten

Jill screamed, too, giving Fran an involuntary bear hug. "Oh, God," she said. "Sorry! I-I was looking for you."

"You found me," Fran gasped.

Jill braced herself with one hand against the wall. "Oh, God," she said again. "You really scared me!"

"*I* scared *you*?" Fran started laughing. And after a moment, so did Jill.

"Any luck?" Fran asked. "With the phones?"

"None. I checked about ten homerooms, too."

"You did?"

"Why? What is it?" Jill asked nervously.

"Nothing, just if one homeroom phone doesn't dial out, then none of them do."

"Oh, right. I'll tell you, I'm really not thinking very clearly. I'm getting too spooked. What about you? You found a phone, right? Tell me you found a working phone."

"No. I didn't."

Jill's eyes went wide with fear. "So what are we going to do?"

"Don't worry," Fran said. "We'll find a phone, I promise you. This whole big place—there's gotta be at least one. C'mon."

They walked side by side down the dark hallway.

"You know, I never liked this school," Jill whispered, "but I never thought it could be this scary."

"Me neither. Where is everyone?"

"Everyone went home," Jill said.

Fran giggled. "No, I mean Jaclyn and Glen and—"

"Oh, right." Jill guffawed. "I don't know. But let me tell you, I liked it a lot better when we were all together."

"Me, too." Fran eyed the heavy girl in the darkness. "How you holding up?"

"Oh, I'm fine. Don't worry. The way I work, the pressure probably won't get to me until we're out of here. Then I'll pass out."

Fran smiled. "Good system."

Jill crossed over to the wall of lockers, peering closely at the numbers. "Here I am. 907. Hold on, okay? I think I've got some more candy in here."

Fran waited while Jill worked her combination. The first time she tried it, the lock didn't open. As Jill tried again, she said softly, "I still feel really embarrassed that I had that anxiety attack in front of everybody."

"Well, don't be," Fran said. "Really. I mean, if anything you should be . . . proud."

"Proud? Oh, right, that's a laugh."

"I'm serious. It takes courage to let your feelings out like that. And . . . and you'll be better off for doing it, too. Really. It's not good to keep stuff like that all bottled up inside."

"You sound like Dr. Shiner," Jill said, opening her locker.

"Dr. Shiner?"

"My shrink." Jill was scrabbling around the clutter on her locker's top shelf. Now she pulled something out. "Want some?"

Fran had to look closely to see what it was—a half-eaten Milky Way bar. "Um, no thanks."

"Aren't you starving?"

"Not really."

Jill's voice became garbled as she stuffed the candy bar into her mouth. "No wonder—you stay so—thin. I could eat—excuse me—a cow."

"We should go by the cafeteria," Fran said. "Maybe we can find some more snacks."

"Great idea!" Jill said.

"Except," Fran said gently, "I think you ought to try calming down first. Then maybe, you know, you won't feel so hungry."

Jill looked at Fran for a moment, then closed and relocked her locker in silence. As they started back down the hall, she said, "Maybe you should be a shrink, Frannie."

Fran snorted. "Right."

"I'm serious. I think you'd be great at it. I mean, you've really got my number pegged, I can tell you."

"Well. Thanks."

Even though she had received the same compliment many times before, Fran felt herself flushing proudly. It was what her mom always said to her after one of their long, late-night heart-to-hearts. *You should be a shrink, Frannie.* But hearing it from Jill made it seem a lot more real, somehow. Mothers complimented everything you did. Friends told you the truth.

Jill stopped by the bubbler for a drink. Fran waited for her to start walking again. But she didn't. "You're so easy to talk to," Jill said, lowering her head, and her voice.

"That comes from being an only child," Fran said. She was also whispering, though she wasn't sure why. "You get to be very good at listening."

Jill was still looking down. "In a way," she said, "I'm kind of glad we're locked in."

"You *are?*"

"Uh huh. At least this way I get to hang out with you a little."

"Aw," Fran said. "That's so sweet."

She felt a stab of pity. Poor Jill. The girl was

a total outcast at Harrison. She had to get locked in the school to get any companionship.

"Well," Fran said, nodding her head down the hall, "I guess we should—"

"Fran?" Jill asked.

"What?"

"Can I tell you something?"

"Sure. I'm a shrink, remember?"

Jill didn't laugh. "You know how I said I was handling this all fine?"

"Uh huh."

Jill suddenly grabbed Fran's arm. "I lied. I'm starting to get really scared."

"There's nothing to worry about," Fran said. "We're just locked in."

"Promise?"

"Promise."

"You'll tell me when I should start to worry?"

"I'll tell you." Fran laughed.

But just then—

The loudspeaker crackled.

"Attention, boys and girls!" boomed the voice. "Attention, boys and girls!"

Fran's mouth dropped open wide. So did Jill's. The two girls spun around, looking up at the ceiling where the voice was coming from.

"It's Mr. Crowley!" whispered Jill, her face twisting with horror.

DEADLY DETENTION

Fran clasped her hands together nervously. "Now you can worry," she told Jill.

It was unnecessary advice. Jill was squeezing Fran's arm so tightly her nails dug into Fran's skin.

"Attention, boys and girls!" Crowley repeated. "This is your detention monitor speaking." He suddenly shouted, "NOW LISTEN UP!"

For a moment, the P.A. system broadcast nothing but the sounds of Crowley's wheezing breath.

"By now," said the Corporal, "I'm sure you've figured out that you're locked in. You can give up trying to find a way out of here because there is none. I found that out when I came here six years ago. Ha-ha. There's no way out!"

Bitter laughter echoed through the halls.

"Yes, ladies and gentlemen," said Crowley, "I'm afraid you're going to have to stay a little later than I thought. . . . In fact, you're going to have to stay *forever*. That's right, kiddies. You're all going to die. One by one."

Eleven

"One by one, ladies and gentlemen," boomed Crowley's voice.

The P.A. system echoed through the entire school. Crowley's horrible voice rasped everywhere, from the gym to the kitchen to the art room—where Glen and Jaclyn were making out.

When they had first split off from the rest of the group, they had started out by doing what they said they'd do—they had searched for Crowley. They'd worked their way down the hallway, checking classroom after classroom. But pretty soon they'd lost interest in finding the teacher. They'd found each other instead.

Things were getting pretty hot and steamy in Classroom #206. At the time the broadcast started, Glen and Jaclyn had been lying on one of the art room's long white wooden drawing tables. But Crowley's speech had kind of ruined the romantic mood.

Glen jumped off the table. He started roam-

DEADLY DETENTION 111

ing around the room in a panic, as if he were looking for a means of escape among the art supplies.

"Hey," Jaclyn said softly. "Get back here."

"Jaclyn," Glen said, his voice an urgent whisper, "we gotta find a way out of here."

"Later," she said in her sexiest voice.

"Later? Are you nuts?" Glen turned sharply, and in the darkness, banged into an easel. It went over with a crash.

Jaclyn tittered. "Easy, big fella."

"Jaclyn, didn't you hear him? He's going to kill us."

"No way, he's just trying to scare us."

"Well, he's doing a pretty good job of it."

From the loudspeakers came only static.

"Lock the door," Jaclyn said.

"What?"

"Lock the door. The lights are out. He'll never find us. Unless—" Her voice took on an even more suggestive air. "Unless I make too much noise."

"Jaclyn!" Glen nearly shouted. "This is serious!"

Jaclyn remained maddeningly calm. "It's not."

Crowley suddenly spoke up again. His slightly garbled voice was incredibly loud in the small room. "Who should I kill first? Let me see. Maybe I should do it alphabetically. Berman, that means you're first, fatso!"

"That sound like joking to you?" Glen asked. His voice was shaky.

"Yup."

"Jaclyn, I'm going to make a run for it. I'm going to try to find a way out, get help. Are you coming with me or not?"

"Not."

"C'monnnn," he cried. "Let's go!"

Jaclyn sat up, stretching languidly. "You're making me very frustrated, you know that, Davis?"

Glen opened the door, staring fearfully out into the darkness. "I said . . . let's go!" he hissed.

"Glen," Jaclyn said sharply. "Wait. Wait! GLEN!"

But Glen was gone.

Crowley's voice was also blasting through the school library, which is where Owen was sitting.

Owen had an unfolded bobby pin in his right hand. Before the P.A. announcement began, he'd been using the pin to try to pick the lock on the librarian's desk phone.

Then Crowley's voice sounded in his ears. Owen put the bobby pin down slowly; his hand was shaking so hard that the pin rattled against the desktop before he was able to drop it.

"Or maybe I'll kill you in order of your grades, from worst to best," said Crowley. "Or . . . maybe I should just kinda—you know—surprise you. Yeah, I think I like that best."

Owen was trembling violently.

Crowley said, "Well, that's all for now. Got to end this broadcast. Got a little work to do."

There were several clicks and then the P.A. system shut off.

Owen waited, expecting the message to continue. "It's a joke, right?" he asked out loud. He was hoping the sound of his own voice might calm him down. But barely any sound came out of his mouth. His throat was bone dry.

All his life, Owen's parents had worried about his health. From the jungle gym onward, they had seemed convinced that he was about to kick the bucket at any second. As a result, Owen had always been convinced that he was about to die. For once, it looked like he was right!

He started snapping his fingers with both hands. Okay, he told himself, Crowley had lost it. But that didn't mean he had *totally* lost it, right? It just meant that Crowley was trying to scare the crap out of them. After all, Mr. Crowley wasn't really a killer. No way. No way. No—

Owen stood up so suddenly and quickly that

he knocked over the librarian's chair. "Oh, Jesus," he said, his voice a scratchy whisper. His little lecture to himself had failed. Panic was bubbling through him; he was drowning in fear. He had to find the others! He couldn't face this alone!

He started to run, but through sheer force of will he slowed himself down to a rapid walk. As resolutely as he could manage, he strode across the library's worn yellow carpet. He stepped out into the hall and, silently yelling the word "CALM!" at himself, reached back to turn off the library lights.

It was an old habit—leave a room, turn off the lights. And if he was going to remain calm, he was going to have to stick to his habits. But this time it meant that he plunged both the library and the hallway outside into darkness. He instantly flicked the library lights on again.

And then he saw it. Across the hallway, in the corner. The large, blue metal box that housed the control panel for the entire school.

His own words came back to him. A couple of snips with a scissor—that's all it would take to shut the place down.

He kept staring at the control panel as if he were hypnotized. He felt as if there were something he was missing.

He realized what it was. It made his heart

DEADLY DETENTION

pound so hard it felt as if it were beating inside his own head.

The control panel's metal door was ajar.

Had he been right? Had Crowley—?

Owen forced himself across the hallway, sliding his feet across the linoleum as if he were moving across thin ice.

The control box was larger and wider than a door, and it ran almost from floor to ceiling. When Owen pulled open the metal door, the hinges creaked loudly.

Inside was a mass of wiring, tiny wires of all different colors like a gigantic serving of spaghetti.

Owen let out a soft moan.

The spaghetti of wires had been cut, right down the middle.

The scissors that had done the cutting were still hanging from the wires inside the box.

Twelve

Crowley had cut the lines! That meant—
This was no joke.
Crowley wasn't just trying to scare them. He was out for blood.

Owen raced back into the library and slammed the door. He locked it, fumbling with the silver button on the doorknob's handle for several moments before he was able to push it in. Then he turned the knob to make sure the door was locked, but that *unlocked* the door, and he had to repeat the whole process a second time.

He ran to the nearest window, raised it, and yelled through the wire mesh, "Police! Help! Help! Police!"

It wasn't until he had shouted "Police!" several more times that he realized how useless this was.

As a senior at Harrison, Owen had finally earned the special senior privilege of going "off-campus" for lunch. For three years he had longed for this privilege so badly. Ached for the chance to get out of the cafeteria and eat his lunch in peace, without fear of the school taking up the chant "Mouse" when he came in and when he left. So when he finally got the privilege, he was determined to use it. Even on cold, rainy days, he had hiked the mile to the Domino's Pizza and the Seven-11.

He knew the route well. To get there, you had to walk past three abandoned factories and through a concrete underpass that smelled of urine and ran under the interstate. If no bullies attacked you in the underpass, you still had to walk several more blocks before coming to the little strip of stores over by Kinderkamack Road.

And that meant, Harrison High was in the middle of nowhere. Owen could scream his head off from the library window. Scream until kingdom come. There was no way anyone would ever hear him. Anyone except Crowley, that is.

He shut the window fast.

Then he whirled around, suddenly expecting Crowley to be right behind him.

Long wooden tables, the gray metal shelves of books, the librarian's desk—the library was still empty, still strangely still.

He whirled back the other way, now expecting Crowley to have snuck up on him from that side. Which would have meant that

Crowley had come through the window. He laughed crazily.

Then he rushed back to the librarian's desk, yanking open the drawer. He found a letter opener and held it up like a knife. He stood there, the opener shaking violently in his hand as if he were trying to dice onions in midair.

He had never been this scared in his entire life. He could barely think.

But he had to think. That's what would get him out of this situation. His brain. He certainly wasn't going to outmuscle Crowley. But he could outthink him. Fifteen fifty on his SATs as a *junior.* He could outthink anybody.

He tried to take deep breaths the way Mike and Fran had coached Jill when she had her anxiety attack back in Room #301. It didn't work. He felt like he was hyperventilating.

Again and again, he told himself he was safe. After all, he had locked the library door.

Right. And Crowley didn't have the key? All teachers and staff had master keys.

Suddenly, Owen started crying. The tears just poured down his cheeks. And then, though it was a struggle, he started to think.

As he paced around the library, he forced himself to review his options.

DEADLY DETENTION 119

He could stay right where he was—turn off the lights, maybe—and wait for Crowley.

Horrible plan. For one thing, the thought of waiting in the dark library terrified him. Besides, once Crowley did come, he would probably just take the letter opener away from him and use it to open his chest.

Owen tried to stop pacing and stand still. But now he started shifting rapidly back and forth from foot to foot, as if he were standing barefoot on hot coals. He went back to pacing. If only he could find the other students, then maybe—

Owen was pacing around so violently that he didn't hear the library door open.

Then the library lights flicked off.

In his shock, Owen dropped the letter opener, the metal blade landing silently on the old yellow carpet.

Suddenly, there was no more time for planning.

Suddenly, Crowley was here.

His heart pounding—bursting—Owen ran for the door. He ran into a table instead, knocking over several volumes of the *Encyclopaedia Britannica* with a tremendous thud.

Owen fell to the floor. The pain in his knee, where he had rammed it into the wooden table leg, was blinding. On the playing field, Owen would have taken an injury such as this as the occasion for a month's absence from gym. That was gym. This was Crowley. Owen was back on his feet as fast as he could scramble. He raced for the door.

A hand grabbed the back of his black sweater.

Screaming, Owen kept running, which meant that his sweater tightened around his neck and choked him.

But an instant later he burst free. He ran down the hallway, flailing his arms and legs like a madman. He was out of breath almost instantly. He stopped, leaning up against the cinderblock wall.

He could hear the footsteps following behind him.

"No! Please!" he gasped.

Then he turned and ran on.

He had no plan now. It was as if his sneakers had taken over. When he came to the hall, his feet turned left without a moment's hesitation. There was no particular reason for turning left, but there was also no time for deciding which way to go. Not a single second.

Turning left led Owen straight to the glass indoor walkway, which in turn led him to the gym.

Good. Maybe Crowley wouldn't bother coming over here. Maybe he'd stick around the main building.

On either side, the walkway's glass walls

looked out onto the black macadam sea of the parking lot. The streetlights and the moonlight showed Owen a surprising thing. Outside the school it was night.

While inside it was hell.

Owen banged through the double doors at the end of the walkway. He stood in the gym's entrance area. He was gasping for breath. He strained his ears, trying to hear over the sound of his own breathing if Crowley was still following him.

When he didn't hear anyone, he almost fell to the cement floor and kissed it with gratitude.

He looked around, hoping he'd spot an exit, a weapon, something. The gym's entrance area, where Owen was now standing, was lined with glass trophy cases and old team photos— row after row of athletes who were probably now aged or dead. Hallways led off on either side, leading to the coaches' offices and locker rooms—boys to the left, girls to the right. Straight ahead, through the red double doors, was the gymnasium itself.

Again without thinking, Owen went right.

Slowly and quietly, the doors at the end of the glass walkway opened a second time.

Owen was running hard, his sneakers pounding against the cold cement floor; he never heard a thing.

He came to the first flight of stairs. The

stairs led up to the track that ran around in an oval above the gym floor, up near the three or four big banners honoring the rare Harrison teams that had won championships. Owen took the cement stairs two at a time.

His only thought—if he could be said to be thinking at all—was to get as far away from Crowley as he could. He rushed out onto the curved wooden track. Down below was the basketball court, the varnished floor shiny in the darkness.

And then he remembered the fire escapes.

At either end of the oval, positioned above the basketball hoops, there was a fire escape door, its EMERGENCY EXIT sign glowing red. Owen squinted. Without his glasses, he couldn't see that far ahead. But he knew from the fuzzy red blobs what the letters said. And in his mind the red letters spelled SALVATION.

If ever someone needed an emergency exit from Harrison High, Owen figured this was it. He started running flat out. The pain in his lungs was searing him with every step. He ignored it. His arms were pumping, his knees coming up high. The exit door loomed closer, closer—his finish line.

And then—

Just as he reached the door—

He felt it.

DEADLY DETENTION 123

It was as if he had broken through the tape that marked the end of track races on TV.

Except whatever this tape was, it caught him across the neck.

He jogged to a halt, feeling suddenly light and rubbery in the legs.

His hands went to his throat.

They came away dark and wet.

Something was gurgling out under his chin. He smelled a funny metallic odor. It was an odor he knew well, because he used to get a nosebleed before every big test. Blood. *His* blood.

He tried to yell, but no sound came out. He tottered—and since the track was curved, his momentum carried him downward, down to the inside of the track, down to the railing.

His hands were still on his neck. He could feel the slippery seam where his throat had been slit, all the way across.

Then his shoes knocked together and—an instant later—he slammed into the wooden railing, hitting it hard. He went right over.

As it turned out, the boy made a really amazing shot.

In fact, if Owen had been *trying* to make this shot, he couldn't have made it in a million years.

As he fell, one of his legs went straight through the basketball hoop.

And that's where he remained, hanging off the hoop like a basketball player who had dunked himself along with the ball.

Thirteen

"Oh, Glennnn. Glenny Glennnnn . . ."

Jaclyn strolled through the dark and deserted third-floor hallway, opening a classroom door here, a classroom door there.

"Come out, come out, wherever you are!"

The only response was the ghostly knocking of steam in the radiator pipes. It sounded like a death rattle.

"C'mon, Glen," she called. "I'm getting tired of playing hide-and-seek. Whereja go?"

She wrinkled her nose in disgust. The way Glen had gone racing out of the room when Crowley started his announcement. What a little chicken. So he wasn't just dumb, but yellow, too. How would she find him now? He was probably sitting under some desk somewhere.

"Glen," she called, pushing open a classroom door with her foot. "I'm telling you," she said into the darkness. "Crowley's just trying to freak us out."

The next door she came to, she yanked it

open, bursting into the room like a cop on a raid, the way they did on TV, imaginary gun drawn in front of her.

Nothing moved inside the classroom. The little light that filtered through the windows glinted off the silver frame of a world globe. She didn't bother to turn on the lights.

She trudged onward until she reached the last classroom on the floor. Which was also the room where tonight's festivities had all started, Classroom #301. Like all the other classrooms she had passed, this room was dark. She opened the door.

She was greeted by the smell of Comet cleanser. She reached around for the light.

And then, two strong hands grabbed her, one hand clapping over her mouth. She was pulled forward into the dark room. The door closed behind her and was kicked shut. There was a click as the door was locked.

Her attacker let her go. She saw who it was.

"There you are, Glen!" she said. "I've been looking all over for you."

"Are you insane?"

"Why?"

"Calling my name like that."

"How else was I going to find you? Where did you go anyway? I've been looking all over for you for about—"

"I was running for my life. Why didn't you follow me?"

DEADLY DETENTION 127

"Oh, stop being so melodramatic. Crowley's just drunk. Turn the lights on," she said.

"No."

"Why not?"

"Crowley will see where we are."

"Good. Then we can stop this game and go home."

Glen grabbed her by the shoulders. "Don't you get it? This isn't a game. Didn't you hear him on the P.A.?"

"Sure I heard him. So what?"

"He's cracked, Jaclyn. He's flipped his lid. He's gone psycho."

Jaclyn giggled. "You're really scared."

"Of course I'm scared!"

"You didn't go to the bathroom in your pants or anything, did you?"

"Shut up!"

"Glen," Jaclyn purred, "have I ever told you how stupid you are?"

Glen was silent. She could see him only dimly, but she could see he was glaring.

"Why would Crowley want to kill us?" she asked.

"How do I know?"

"Well think. There's no reason, that's why. No reason in the world. He's not that crazy, Glen."

"What are you talking about? You said it yourself, how crazy he is."

"Mmm hmm. But why would he *kill* us?"

"Because—because of all those things you said. About how he hates kids . . . because of what his son did. You know."

"Sure," Jaclyn said. "That's why he hates kids. All grownups hate kids, Glen. But they don't go around killing them."

Jaclyn put her arms around Glen's neck; he pried them off and pushed her away. "Jaclyn, you can say whatever you like. I still heard him on the P.A. He sounded pretty serious."

"Yeah," Jaclyn agreed. "He's really lost it this time. I'm going to make sure he gets fired, believe me."

She put her arms around Glen's neck again. "But what are you worrying about? The door's locked, right? As long as we stay in here, we're safe."

"He probably has the key."

She massaged the tight muscles in Glen's powerful neck. She whispered in his ear, "Don't you think you could handle Crowley, if he tries to come in here? I know you can. You'll protect me, won't you, Glen?"

"Jaclyn, I really think we—"

She silenced him with a kiss, long and probing.

"Mmm," he said, "Jac—"

She kissed him a second time. She didn't stop until she had to take a breath. "On second thought," she said, "let's leave the lights off, just like you said."

"Jaclyn, this is crazy. We've got to get out of here."

But he didn't sound as convinced as before, and after the next kiss he sounded even less convinced.

She moved away from him.

"What are you doing?" he asked.

There was the sound of vinyl crinkling. "Just making myself comfortable."

Glen's voice came out several notes lower than usual. "Where are you?"

"On Crowley's desk."

"Oh, God."

"It's the perfect spot. After all, we spent the whole afternoon scrubbing it so nice and clean."

"Jaclyn, you're out of control, you know that? Can't you ever get enough?"

"No, Glen, I just can't seem to." He heard snaps unsnapping, zippers unzipping. "Come here," Jaclyn ordered.

"Oh, God," Glen said again. But he started shuffling forward, feeling in front of him with both hands; he bumped into one of the student desks, hard. Jaclyn giggled.

Then he reached the teacher's desk. Groping with both hands, he found himself holding Jaclyn's legs; the feel of Jaclyn's soft, sheer tights felt electric against his palms.

"Hi," she said softly.

"Hi."

"Glen?"

"What?"

"I know you're mad at me and everything, and I'm pretty mad at you, but the thing is, I still want you."

He grunted.

"I'm yours, Glen," she said, even more softly.

"Okay," he said.

He was climbing up onto the large gray desk when the doorknob turned—hard.

And then there was pounding.

"Don't get it!" Jaclyn hissed. She had both arms around Glen's head, her long fingernails digging into his scalp, pulling him down toward a kiss. Pushing hard, he raised his head, listening.

"Glen? Jaclyn?" It was a girl's voice, a desperate whisper. "Are you in there?"

"It's that jerkface, Weber," Jaclyn muttered. Loudly, she called, "We're busy. Come back later!"

Glen pried her hands loose. "C'mon, Jaclyn we've got to let her in."

Jaclyn sat up as Glen headed toward the door. "I hate you," she said into the darkness.

Then the door opened, letting in the gloomy light from the safety lights in the hall. The door closed again.

DEADLY DETENTION 131

"Hi—it's—me," Fran said. She was short of breath. And then, all at once, she started crying. Glen held her.

The feel of being in his big strong arms was even more amazing to Fran than her sudden burst of tears. "Sorry," she murmured. "This is all just so—so—"

"So ridiculous," Jaclyn finished for her.

Fran sniffled. Glen wasn't holding her so close anymore, but he was still holding her. "Why do you have the lights off?" she asked.

"Why do you think?" Jaclyn asked back.

"It's safer," Glen whispered.

Jaclyn laughed. Glen sighed. "Jaclyn thinks it's all just a prank," he said.

"Oh, wow," Fran said. "I hope you're right. I've been walking around and around and I couldn't find anyone, and I started to think—" She sniffed once more, then got control of herself. "So you guys are okay?"

"We were until you interrupted," Jaclyn said coldly.

"Is there anyone else in here?" Fran asked. "Owen? Jill? Mike?"

"Just me and Jaclyn," Glen said.

"Now you get the idea?" asked Jaclyn, even more coldly.

"Oh," said Fran. "Sorry." There was an awkward silence. Glen finally let go of her. The skin of her bare arms where his hands had rested felt red-hot. "So where is everybody?" she asked.

"Everyone must be hiding," Glen said.

"Yeah," Jaclyn said. "And this is *our* hiding place, so why don't you go find one of your own?"

"Jaclyn," Fran said, "don't you think we should stick together?"

"No, I don't."

"Fran's right," Glen said firmly. Then, to Fran, he added, "Don't worry. You're staying here."

There was an ominous silence from over by the teacher's desk.

"I was with Jill when we heard the announcement," Fran explained. "She got totally hysterical and started running and I lost her and—"

She felt the tears coming on again; she was starting to hiccough. But then Glen was holding her again. They stood together in a silent embrace. Fran wondered if the darkness of the room would shield the embrace from Jaclyn.

"If you don't let go of her pretty soon, there's going to be two murderers on the loose around here," Jaclyn called.

Glen let go. "She's upset," he told Jaclyn, by way of explanation.

"I'm all right now," Fran said. "Thanks."

Then she heard it. Out in the hallway. Loud footsteps. Followed by wailing.

DEADLY DETENTION

"It's Jill!" Fran whispered.

Glen unlocked the door. "Berman! Over here."

The large, heavyset girl barreled into the classroom like a fullback hitting the hole. She was weeping. Glen closed and locked the door behind her. This time it was Fran, not Glen, who did the hugging.

"It's okay," Fran said. "You're safe now, Jill. You found us. And the door's locked. It's locked! Jill—you're okay!"

"Why are the lights out?" Jill asked frantically. "Why are the lights out? Why are—"

She kept repeating the question until the lights flicked on.

"I'm only leaving these on for a second, Jill," Glen said. "Get a grip on yourself."

Jill blinked, her long lashes wet with tears.

Fran blinked, too, her eyes adjusting to the sudden bright light.

Standing by the door, his hand still on the lightswitch, was Glen.

Standing right next to Fran, whimpering softly, was Jill.

Sitting on the desk, lazily buttoning up her lacy white blouse, was Jaclyn.

"We're all going to die," said Jill, in between sobs.

"That's true," Jaclyn said. "But not tonight. I figure we've all got another sixty years. Except you, Jill, the way you eat."

"Don't listen to her," Fran told Jill. "As long as we stick together, we'll be all right. I promise you."

"Crowley . . . Crowley is a maniac," Jill said.

"That's for sure," Glen said.

Jaclyn pushed off the desk and stood up. "Here's what we should do. We'll all stick together, like Fran says. We'll go through the school until we find him. And then we'll confront him. He's probably drunk out of his mind. If things get out of hand, Glen here can knock him out. Glen's dumb, but he's strong. Aren't you, Glen?"

Glen looked away.

"The point is, Jill," Jaclyn continued, "Crowley wants you to do exactly what you're doing—cry like a little baby. When he sees we're not scared, this whole game is going to stop being fun for him, and he'll drop it."

Fran studied Jaclyn for a moment. "You may be right."

"Of course I'm right."

Jill wiped her nose loudly on the back of her hand. "You're sure it's just a game?"

"Positive," Jaclyn said.

Jill looked questioningly at Fran.

"I can't believe Crowley would really hurt us," Fran said as gently as she could.

Jill looked at Glen.

He nodded cheerlessly. "We'll be fine."

DEADLY DETENTION

And then Jill looked at the blackboard.

Her face went paper white. She swayed like she was about to faint.

"Look!" she finally managed to say, pointing at the board.

She was pointing at Crowley's list.

THE STUPID CLUB.

Owen's name had been erased.

Fourteen

"Owen's gone!" Jill wailed. "He's gone, he's gone, he's gone."

"Stop saying that!" Jaclyn snapped. "How stupid can you get? Just because the Corporal wiped his name off the board, you think he's dead?"

Jill nodded, her mouth open, fresh tears glistening at the corners of her eyes.

"C'mon," Jaclyn said. "Let's go." With a sigh—as if she were tired of having to be the smart one—she started for the door.

She turned to look at the three other teenagers. "My plan is still the only idea that makes sense," she said. "Anyone have something better?" No one responded. "I didn't think so."

She turned and continued toward the door. She didn't get far.

Because just then, the P.A. system crackled to life once more.

"Hello, kiddies. Itttttt's Mr. Crowley."

The four teenagers in Room #301 all stood

rooted to the spot, staring at each other in horror.

"Well, kiddies, you'll be glad to know that I've finished part of the job. Yes, that's right, ladies and gentlemen. One of you is," Crowley's voice suddenly rose to a shout, "DEAD!"

A wheeze-filled pause followed.

"Yup. Looks like one of you won't have to worry about getting detention anymore!"

More wheezing. Some coughing. Then the Corporal said, "One down. Five to go."

The P.A. clicked off.

Jill was weeping openly now.

Even Jaclyn looked a little pale. There were little red splotches in the center of her cheeks, as if she'd been slapped. But when she spoke she sounded calm. "Good," she said.

"Good?" Glen asked, his brown eyes wide with wonder.

"Now we know where Crowley is. He's in the principal's office. Let's go talk to him."

She opened the door. The other three teenagers didn't move.

"Glen," she said. "You're not going to make me go alone, are you?"

"Of course not."

"Don't leave me here," Jill cried, as Jaclyn and Glen went out the door. She rushed after them.

Jaclyn stuck her head back into the room. She smiled at Fran in a fake and icy way. "Why don't you stick around here and finish up cleaning off the graffiti?"

"I'm coming," Fran said grimly.

But when they reached the principal's office, it was empty.

"Well, he *was* here, that's for sure," Jaclyn said. "This is the only place you can broadcast from."

"Now what do we do?" Glen asked.

"I don't know, Glen," Jaclyn said brightly. "Why don't you think of something for once?"

"I don't know," he said thoughtfully.

"Good thinking," she said.

Jill was huddled in the corner. "We'll never get out of here," she wailed.

"Maybe you won't, but I will," Jaclyn said.

Fran was checking the office's front door. "I don't think we should stay here. This door only locks with a key. And Crowley's got that key for sure."

"Of course we're not staying here," Jaclyn said. "I'm telling you, once we find Crowley, this whole thing will all be over."

"Our whole lives will be over," Jill said.

"Where's Mike?" Fran suddenly asked, looking worried.

"Mike," Jaclyn said. "Hey, I forgot all about the Mikester. Where *is* old Mike?"

"He's dead, too," Jill said numbly. Her lower lip was bluish, as if she'd just come out of a freezing pool. "He's dead, just like Owen."

"Oh, can it, would you?" Jaclyn spat out.

"Jaclyn," Fran said. "Leave her alone. You're only making things worse."

Jaclyn made a face of mock pity. "Sorry. Now let's see . . . if I were Mike, where would I be right now?"

"In the gym, pumping iron," guessed Glen.

Jaclyn put an arm around Glen's shoulder. "Isn't he something, ladies and gentleman? Isn't that a brilliant guess? Mr. Crowley is stalking around the school, playing psycho killer, and Glen thinks Mike is working out."

Glen turned pink. "He's always working out," he said defensively.

Fran looked out the window. From the principal's office you could see about half of the round gym building. "Oh, my God!" Fran said. "Glen's right. The lights are on in the gym!"

They all moved to the window to look at what Fran was seeing.

It was true. The gym was a blaze of light.

Fifteen

Jaclyn pulled the office door open wide. "Let's go."

Fran hesitated a moment. Then she started after Jaclyn, and soon they were all running down the hallway together.

"Mike!" Jaclyn shouted. "Owen!"

"Shut up!" Glen cried.

Jill slowed down to a trot, clutching her sides. Fran stopped to wait for her. "Hold on," she called to Jaclyn.

Jaclyn waited, jogging in place. "C'mon!" she hissed.

Fran took Jill's arm and helped her down the hall. They turned left, right, then headed through the glass walkway. Jill held her Bart Simpson watch up close to her glasses. "Anyone know . . . what time it is? I can't . . . see my watch."

"Ten after eight," said Glen.

"My parents will be so worried," Jill said. Her voice caught like she was going to start crying again. "They won't know where I am!"

"Jill," Fran said firmly. "We've got bigger things to worry about at the moment."

"I know," Jill said. "But do you think maybe they'll call the cops?"

"I doubt it," Jaclyn said. "And what if they do? Why would anyone think of looking for us here?"

Jill thought about this. "What about your parents, Frannie? Maybe *they'll* call the cops."

"My parents are both out of town, visiting my aunt," Fran said.

"And I was going to Glen's house to study after school, " Jaclyn said. "They don't expect me home for another hour."

"My parents never know if I'm home or not," Glen said miserably.

"HEY, MR. CROWLEY!" Jaclyn shouted as she pushed through the double doors into the gym.

She was still shouting when Glen, Fran, and Jill pushed through the doors after her. Glen grabbed her. "Stop that!"

Jaclyn pushed him off. "I'll shout if I want to shout."

She shouted for several more seconds, just to make her point.

Under cover of all that shouting, a figure pushed open the double doors behind them. Thanks to the noise, no one heard him. He stood in the shadows, watching and grinning.

Fran placed her hands on the handles to

the large red doors that led into the gymnasium itself.

"Something tells me we shouldn't go in there," Jill said. She was cowering right behind Fran.

"Why not?" Fran asked. But she didn't open the doors.

"Just a hunch," Jill said. Fran could feel the girl shaking.

"Oh, for God's sake," Jaclyn said. "C'mon, Weber, let's go. Open the door."

"I wouldn't do that if I were you," said a deep voice, right behind them.

Screaming, they all jumped straight up in the air.

The figure standing right behind them fell to the floor, holding his stomach and laughing. "Gotcha!" Mike cried.

"You . . . you jerk!" Jaclyn lunged toward the fallen wrestler. She raised one orange boot, pulling it back as she prepared to kick him. He rolled away.

"I've been looking all over for you guys," he said. "Where've you been?"

"Having a party," Jaclyn said. "Where do you think we've been?"

"Have you seen Owen?" Fran asked Mike quickly.

"I haven't seen a soul," Mike said. "I was starting to get pretty weirded out, too."

DEADLY DETENTION 143

"What about Crowley?" Glen asked. "Have you seen him?"

"He said he hasn't seen anyone," Jaclyn said. "Get it?"

"I think Crowley went home," Mike said, sitting up.

"Oh, right," Jaclyn said. "Then who's broadcasting over the P.A? His ghost?"

Mike started laughing all over again, but Jaclyn turned and stalked into the gym.

"What about Binder?" Fran asked Mike.

"He went home, too," Mike said, still laughing. "We're really locked in."

"That's not funny," Jill said.

"Hello?" Jaclyn was calling loudly inside the gym. "Anybody home?"

She had left the gym doors open behind her. They all followed her inside.

The gym and the bleachers were empty.

Then Glen looked up and pointed. "Hey," he said.

The scoreboard was lit. The score read: HOME-0, VISITORS-1.

Mike whistled. *"I* thought I was the practical joker around here. Who's trying to horn in on my territory?"

"Oh, get out," Jaclyn said, "you did that and you know it."

"Did not."

"Did," Jaclyn said, adding quickly, "infinity!"

"Mike," Fran said. Her green eyes were

filled with fear. "This has gone far enough. If you did it, you better say."

Mike shook his head. "I didn't," he said with a shrug.

They were standing right under the basketball hoop.

"Hey," Mike said, taking off his white cap. He studied the cap, amazed to see that several small red polka-dots were staining the soft material.

Jaclyn was looking down at the puddle of dark wetness she had stepped into. "What the—"

Fran looked at Mike's face, then spun around. And then she looked up at the basketball hoop—

And started screaming.

It was a piercing cry that echoed through the empty gymnasium.

Her cry was soon joined by the screams of the four others.

And then they were all racing out of the gym.

Sixteen

Jill ran across the gym floor and out the back entrance. Still running, she turned right and circled past the girls' locker rooms, the coaches' offices, and the training room. When she had made it back to the gym's entrance area she paused, gasping for breath. It was only then that she realized the other students had not followed her. She was alone.

"Fran!" was the first name she screamed. Then, "Mike!"

Hearing no answer, she started running again. She didn't stop until she was back in the main building.

It was the hardest and longest she had ever run in her life. Every breath was agony. It didn't feel like any air was going in. Her lungs felt locked.

Still, she forced herself to keep moving. Desperately, she tried several office doors. Finding them all locked, she turned down another hallway and banged into the cafeteria, flicking on every lightswitch she could find.

She ran past row after row of long, white, ugly Formica tables. She fell twice. She kept screaming, the sound pouring out of her in short bursts. She wasn't even aware of when it would start.

Owen, Owen—the sight of him, hanging from the backboard—so horrible, so unreal. It was like one of those stunts the cheerleading team pulled before a big game. Setting up a dummy dressed like a player from the enemy school and hanging him in the cafeteria for kids to punch and kick.

Only this was really Owen.

And he was really dead.

She started running again, stopped again almost at once, slowed down by the knifing pain in her side.

She half-pushed, half-fell through the swinging black doors into the kitchen and was hit—

By the smell. Along with ammonia, the large kitchen smelled vaguely of school meals—sour milk, peanut butter, burgers, sloppy joes, shepherd's pie. Every meal at Harrison was pretty horrible, all the kids said so. But Jill liked all food—even bad food had its pleasures. And right now, right in the middle of her terror, there was something comforting to her about these familiar odors.

DEADLY DETENTION

She hurried to the back of the kitchen. Sobbing, she pressed herself up against a wall of steel cupboards.

Owen was dead! Owen was dead! It was too awful a thing to comprehend. And . . . and Crowley was deranged. Crowley was a killer.

Jill's next thought shook her even harder. She had only gotten detention once in her life. Now she was going to die for it.

"No!" She mouthed the word.

She had to defend herself.

But how?

In the center of the room was the long stainless steel worktable which the cooks used to prepare the daily slop they served at Harrison. And hanging above that table from a long metal strip was a row of huge kitchen knives and cleavers. One of the cleavers was missing, leaving a gap in the row like a missing tooth.

Jill stayed where she was. She couldn't move. Her whole body felt like one big vat of Jell-O that wasn't set. Besides, she knew she'd be useless with a weapon. In her current state, she doubted she could even grip the knife's handle.

Her fear was worse than all her anxiety attacks combined. It was as if she were so afraid that she couldn't even feel the fear. Couldn't feel a thing.

Then she became aware of the sound.

The steady drip, drip, drip of one of the faucets into the huge metal sink. She turned her head sharply, peering across the kitchen through her thick glasses. Even the dripping terrified her, as if the drip of a leaky faucet was yet another threat to her life.

In a way, it was.

For Owen, it was.

Drip, drip, drip. Back in the gym, his body was dripping the last of its blood onto the gym floor.

It was hopeless, she realized. She would just wait here until Crowley came and got her.

Oddly enough, she took comfort in her resignation.

Maybe it was because Crowley was a teacher, an adult. Jill desperately wanted to see an adult right about now. Even if the adult was a psycho killer, somehow that still ranked in her brain as adult supervision.

Jill began to blubber, her shoulders going up and down as they did when she laughed, but violently now, in horrible heaves. Under the extreme stress, a truth had cracked open inside her. The truth was that if Crowley wanted her dead, she wanted to die.

Anything to please.

Anything but that feeling of letting down the adults.

"Oh," she said over and over again. "Oh."

She kept weeping, the tears leaking down around the bottom of her glasses.

She couldn't believe that more tears kept coming out after she had already done so much crying. It was astonishing how much water her body could store and send out through her eyes.

She took off her glasses, wiped her face, then put her glasses back on.

Well, she was still here, still alive.

Not only that, she was hungry.

In one of the pamphlets they gave you at O.A. there was a listing of all the different reasons people ate. They ate to feel safe, to feel comforted, to feel loved. They ate to block out fear, sadness, loneliness. They ate to get attention, they ate to avoid attention, they ate, they ate, they ate. The first time Jill read the pamphlet, she was stunned. She ate for every single reason they listed.

Well, now she could add a new item to that list. She ate to get over her fear of psycho killers.

She scanned the room. The shelves were stocked with generic silver tins and cans, huge industrial-sized portions of all the basic staples such as vegetable oil and Crisco. Then her eyes found something more promising.

The door to the walk-in fridge.

It was a huge wooden door with metal crossbars and latches and knobs, like the door to some medieval castle. She knew the refrigerator wasn't locked. Because the door was slightly ajar. And if the door had a lock on the inside . . . she might have just found the perfect hiding place for herself! A place where she'd be safe until help arrived!

In the middle of her horror, Jill almost laughed. This one time, her stomach might have saved her life.

The fridge door was heavy. She had to struggle to pull it open. Cold air enveloped her as she stepped inside.

The first thing she checked was the lock. Sure enough, there was a large metal bolt that slid right across the door and into the wall.

She pulled the door shut with both hands, then worked the bolt feverishly until she was finally able to slip it home.

There! She was safe! She stood there, her chest heaving, letting the cold air wash over her like relief.

She was safe. But she was also in the dark.

Didn't they have a light in these refrigerators?

Well, if they did, it was broken. She had locked herself into a cold and clammy chamber of pitch darkness.

That was still a lot better than roaming around the halls of Harrison with mad Crowley on the loose.

She turned around. She had been in walk-in

fridges like this before. Last summer when she was working at BJ's ice cream parlor, she had had to go in and out of the freezer all the time. She was fired when the manager caught her in the freezer, finishing off a half-gallon of Rocky Road Caramel Surprise.

So she knew what this fridge was like, even without seeing it. It would be a large wooden room, lined top to bottom with food.

All her life Jill had relied on two main strategies for dealing with fear—eating and sleeping. She figured she could use both strategies now. She would eat and eat until she had stuffed herself, and then she would go to sleep on the floor and—

An awful thought occurred to her.

Was it so chilly in here that she would freeze to death by morning?

Not if she covered herself with boxes and other stuff. She'd seen a guy make a nest in the woods in this wilderness adventure movie on TV last week. In the movie the man had survived by eating snow.

She wouldn't have to resort to that. She could have a feast. She started groping around. She was feeling along the shelves for food when—

She heard the sound.

A rustle, from the back end of the fridge.

Oh, God.

Were there rats in here?

Well, she wasn't going outside, rats or no rats. She'd just have to pray that if there were rats, they had enough to eat already and wouldn't bother with a human.

She was beginning to feel a little calmer now, despite the threat of rodents. After all, she had an iron bolt and a massive door in between her and Crowley, the biggest rat of all. She sighed over and over. Then she went back to feeling along the shelves. Her hands found a large crinkly wrapper of wax paper. She unwrapped it.

Inside was a human arm.

She screamed, but only briefly, for then she realized what she was really touching and got control of herself.

It was a huge rectangular hunk of that yellow processed American cheese she loved so much. Mommy food, she called it, the kind of stuff her mother always used to give her when she was sick.

Her mouth started watering. She peeled off several slices of cheese and stuffed them into her mouth.

Delicious.

Moving farther back into the freezer, she found a large tin. She unscrewed the lid and dipped her hand inside, her fingers finding something soft and gushy. The smell had already hit her nostrils even before she brought

DEADLY DETENTION 153

the large glop into her mouth. Peanut butter . . . Mmmmmm.

It wasn't easy swallowing handfuls of peanut butter without bread or anything to wash it down. But she managed.

She moved farther back into the fridge, the cold starting to get to her now so that she stooped and tried to snuggle within the folds of her bulky red sweater. She found salami (she ate eight slices), raw hamburger (she spat it out), and leftover salmon croquettes (she ate four).

Like a drug, the food in her stomach was beginning to take effect, comforting her, soothing her, putting her in a sleepy daze. She started to daydream about the articles the newspapers would write about tonight's murder. Maybe they'd tell about the clever resourceful girl who hid in the freezer. Print her picture. A nice picture, showing just her face. She'd get all sorts of attention, be interviewed on TV, shake hands with the governor. Her parents would be so proud. And then, best of all, a college would call—Harvard, Yale, or Princeton.

"We read about your ordeal, Jill. Boy were you clever! In fact, you were so clever, we'd like to offer you a full scholarship. Correction, we want to pay you a *salary* just to come to our school. What do you say? Please, Jill? Pleasy-pleasy please with ice cream on top?"

She belched loudly, then put her hand over her mouth as she suddenly remembered the danger that could be lurking right outside the fridge door.

Her body tensed, listening for sounds from the kitchen. After all, Crowley might have a gun. Maybe he could shoot off the lock, or shoot her through the fridge door.

She kept listening.

She didn't hear any sounds coming from the kitchen.

The sounds she heard came from a different direction.

They came from *behind* her.

What she heard was a sudden rustle.

And then—

A hand grabbed a thick handful of her brown hair and jerked her head straight back.

Seventeen

Jaclyn was running through the hall toward the cafeteria when she heard the scream.

She burst through the cafeteria doors.

The huge dining space was empty.

Then she heard it again. The sound was coming from the kitchen.

It was Mike, bellowing like a stuck pig.

She had once been to a wrestling match where Mike got pinned (which was a very rare event). As the opponent pressed his back and shoulders down onto the mat, Mike had let out a scream of frustration and terror and pain that could be heard, students later claimed, all the way back in the locker rooms.

Well, this scream was just like that other scream, only ten times worse.

Jaclyn raced into the kitchen. Mike was standing there, his purple T-shirt wet with sweat as if he really were in the middle of a wrestling match.

"What?" she asked breathlessly.

She followed his gaze.

On the burners of the huge stove sat a bunch of tall, silver spaghetti pots.

Hanging out from under the lid of one of the pots was a human hand.

In the distance, the cafeteria doors slammed—once, twice.

A moment later, Glen ran into the room, followed by Fran.

"What is it?" Glen asked. He was carrying a pointer he had picked up in one of the classrooms; he was holding it like a spear.

Jaclyn couldn't speak. She turned back toward the stove.

"Oh, no," Fran murmured. "No!"

Setting the pointer in the corner, Glen moved forward, toward the pots.

"Don't touch it," Jaclyn cried.

Glen ignored her. He lifted the lid of the pot. The hand, which had been balanced precariously, fell with a light thud onto the stovetop. Still strapped to the bleeding stump of a wrist was a girl's Bart Simpson watch with a pink leather band.

Fran, Mike, and Jaclyn all stepped backward, so that they clumped together in a little knot.

"Jesus," said Glen.

"Don't touch it!" Jaclyn warned.

"I won't," Glen said, tears forming in his soft brown eyes. Fran could feel tears welling

DEADLY DETENTION 157

up in her eyes, too. Then Glen reached for one of the other pots on the stove.

"Glen!" Jaclyn yelled. "Don't."

Glen glanced back at her, his brown eyes swimming with tears now, but somehow expressionless at the same time.

"Let's get out of here!" Jaclyn cried.

Ignoring her, Glen lifted the silver lid and looked inside the pot.

For a moment, he was silent, just staring in. It was so quiet in the room, it was as if no one were breathing. The only sound was the drip of the leaky faucet. Then Glen reached into the pot.

When he pulled out what was inside the pot, Jaclyn rushed from the room. Fran was right behind her. From the cafeteria came the sound of retching.

Glen was holding Jill's bloody head.

Her eyes were bulging, her mouth and cheeks were smeared with bits of salami and cheese.

Mike came rushing out of the kitchen, his hand over his mouth. Glen followed closely behind him.

The two girls were by the far wall. Fran was struggling to open one of the windows. Both girls' faces were as white as the bellies of the frogs that swam in jars of formaldehyde in Mr. Crowley's lab.

Again carrying his pointer, Glen made a

wide circle around the spot where one of the girls had tossed her cookies. So did Mike. They joined the girls at the window. It was several moments before anyone could speak.

"We've got to find a way out of here," Mike said. His voice was quiet and shaky and his face was almost as pale as the two girls.'

"There's no way," Glen said. "I checked."

"There's got to be," Mike said.

"I think we should all split up," Jaclyn said suddenly. Her voice was small and tight.

"No," Fran said. "Bad idea." She was wiping her mouth with the back of her hand again and again. She looked down. She could see little flecks of throw-up on her left saddle shoe. Her stomach heaved. "We've got to stay . . . together," she mumbled.

Jaclyn said, "That's crazy. It'll be harder for that maniac Crowley to find us if we go off on our own."

"No," Fran said, more firmly this time. "You said it yourself, Jaclyn. There's safety in numbers."

"Frannie's right," said Glen. He crossed his strong arms.

"Oh, what do you know, lamebrain," Jaclyn cried, sudden fury messing up her pretty features.

Glen was breathing deeply, as if he'd been running hard. "What do I know? I know that we should stay together, like Fran says. And I know something else. We *are* going to stay together. No more running off again, Jaclyn."

"Oh, you're just so stupid!" Jaclyn shrieked. "All of you!"

Fran stared at her in surprise. The girl had always been nasty, but very controlled. Her usual composure was all gone. The mask had completely dropped. She was a changed girl.

As calmly as she could, Fran said, "Look. Owen died and Jill died when they were *alone*. There's four of us, including two strong guys. If we stay together, we've got a chance."

Without a word, Mike started toward the kitchen.

"Where are *you* going?" Jaclyn snapped.

"I thought you said we should split up?" he said, grinning insanely.

Jaclyn's eyes narrowed. "Cut the crap! Where are you going?"

Mike shrugged. "I've got an idea."

He disappeared through the swinging doors into the kitchen. They all waited, eyes fixed on the doors. Just as the doors finally stopped swinging, Mike pushed through again, coming back the other way. He was carrying a large silver pot.

Jaclyn pressed back against the wall. "Mike, are you crazy? Keep that thing away from me."

"Out of the way," Mike said. Using the pot as a battering ram, he shattered a window.

Then he started ramming the metal pot against the wire mesh and bars.

He grunted and groaned with the effort. Glen watched for a moment, then joined in, using his pointer to try to poke holes in the mesh. He succeeded only in cracking the pointer in half, leaving a jagged wooden edge.

Fran gasped.

Mike stopped, pot held aloft. He and Glen and Jaclyn were all staring at her.

"Look!" Fran said, pointing.

From this window she could see only a sliver of the parking lot.

"What?" Jaclyn said.

"The parking lot," Fran said.

"Yeah?" Jaclyn hissed. "So?"

"The parking lot!" Fran yelled. "Look!"

"I don't see a thing," said Glen.

"Exactly," Fran said, trembling.

"What are you talking about?" cried Jaclyn shrilly. "What? What? What?"

"Those are the teachers' parking spaces," Fran said. She bit her chapped lower lip, bit it hard.

Jaclyn pushed her shoulder roughly. "So?"

"So," Fran said, "Crowley's car isn't there."

Jaclyn thought about this for a second. So did Mike. He put down the pot.

"So?" Jaclyn said again, but she said it more softly this time.

"So Crowley *is* gone," said Fran.

"Well, *that's* good news," Glen said with a nervous grin. "Isn't it?"

"Seems kind of strange, doesn't it?" Fran asked.

"Yeah," said Mike. "Why . . . why would he just go?"

"Exactly," Fran said. There was a draft of icy air from the broken window hitting her back. But that wasn't the reason she started shaking.

"All right, Weber," Jaclyn said. "Let's have it. What are you getting at?"

Fran's eyes were wet with tears but her face was serious and composed. "It doesn't make sense that Crowley would kill two of us and then go home."

"What?" Jaclyn's chin was trembling. "And it makes sense that Crowley would chop up Jill Berman into little pieces? That makes sense?"

"Say what you're thinking," Mike told Fran.

Fran turned both hands palm up, her bracelets jangling; she stared down into her hands as if they held her thoughts. "I'm thinking," she said softly, "that the killer is one of us."

Eighteen

"You're out of your mind," Jaclyn said. "We all heard him on the P.A. It was Crowley for su—"

She stopped mid-word, her ice-blue eyes locking on Mike.

The stocky boy's face was crinkled in its usual grin, but behind the smile there was fear. "What?"

"Yeah, what?" Glen repeated dumbly. "What's going on?"

Jaclyn's eyes were glowing. "You do an awfully good Crowley imitation, don't you, Mike?"

"Gee, thanks, Jaclyn," he said, "but I'm not sure what that has to do with anything."

Jaclyn stalked toward him. He back-pedalled. She poked his chest, hard, as she spat out her accusation. "It was *you!*"

"No way," Mike said.

"Why didn't I think of it till now?" Jaclyn said. "You did the imitation for us, right in class."

"Yeah. I was goofing around. So were you," he reminded her.

"Two kids are dead, Mike!" Jaclyn yelled. "You call that goofing around?"

Mike was sweating harder; the dots of perspiration on his purple shirt were starting to connect into large, dark patches. "Just because I do a good Crowley imitation," he said, "doesn't mean—"

Jaclyn whirled to face Glen and Fran. "That last announcement we heard. Everyone was in the room. Except Mike. Right?"

Fran nodded gravely. She was trying not to look at Mike directly. He looked totally and completely guilty.

Glen thought for a second, then said, "Yeah, that's right. Everyone was in the room except Mike. Wait a minute. Owen wasn't there either."

"Yeah, right," Jaclyn said to Glen. "Well, we know Owen didn't make the announcement. Right, genius?"

Glen looked away, his face reddening.

Jaclyn turned back to Mike. "That leaves you, Morricone."

Mike moistened his lips and cleared his throat several times. His throat sounded dry as dust. "Okay," he said. "I admit it. I . . . I did make those announcements."

Jaclyn let out a huge dramatic gasp. "Murderer," she said. Her eyes were glittering like jewels.

"But—but I didn't do anything else," Mike rushed on. "I swear. I just thought, since we were all stuck here and since I was sure Crowley went home—well, it just seemed like too good a joke to pass up. But I really thought you'd all know it was me for sure. And I was going to tell you it was me. I swear."

"When?" Jaclyn snapped. "When were you going to tell us? Tomorrow?"

"No, when I caught up with you at the gym. But then—"

"But then we found Owen," Jaclyn said.

"Right," Mike said. Finished with his rush of words, he stared at each of their faces in turn, like an accused criminal waiting for a jury's verdict.

Fran studied Mike's face. He gave her a sickly smile. "I believe him," she said.

"Weber, you are so naive," Jaclyn said. "Look at him. He did it. You can tell just by his face that he's—" Jaclyn's face went pale again. She turned back to Mike. "Wait a minute," she said. "You made that second announcement, too? The one about one of us being dead?"

Mike nodded.

Jaclyn whirled back to face the others. "That proves it. He knew that Owen was killed."

Drops of sweat beaded on Mike's forehead and ran down into his eyebrows. "Wow. Guys. Listen, okay? I know it's a big coincidence. But I just said that to keep the joke going. You gotta believe me. I mean, you all saw me in the gym when we found him. I was just as scared as everyone else."

"You were faking!" Jaclyn cried.

"Wait a minute, wait a minute," Fran said. "You're overlooking something huge here, Jaclyn."

"Oh, yeah? What's that?"

"You haven't said why. *Why* would Mike kill Jill? Or Owen?"

"Yeah," said Glen. "Why?" He said it to Jaclyn, not Mike.

Jaclyn threw up her hands. "That's easy. Mikey here's not the world's happiest guy. He went crazy. Found some scapegoats. Two dorks, two outcasts. Everybody hated Jill and Owen."

"Maybe you hate them, but I don't," Fran said. "Didn't," she corrected herself. Fighting back tears, she said, "And Mike didn't hate them either. No way. He was one of the few people in school who was nice to them."

Mike's smile broadened. "Thank you," he mouthed.

Jaclyn appeared to be thinking—hard. She was moving around Mike in a circle, her eyes on him every second. "All right," she said. "So you tell us, Mike. Why did you kill them?"

"I didn't kill them," Mike said. "I didn't touch them. C'mon, Jaclyn, you know me better than that."

Jaclyn stopped short, studying his face. "So that's it," she said with a smile of triumph.

"That's what?" Mike asked, but he was looking more and more nervous, more and more guilty.

"It's because of me," Jaclyn said.

"I have no idea what you're talking—"

Jaclyn turned back to Fran. "Mike is in love with me."

"Hah!" said Mike.

"Always has been, always will be." Jaclyn gave a quick toss of her wavy blond hair. "Like every other dumb slob in this school."

"Jaclyn," said Mike, "you're fantasizing again."

"I dumped Mike for Cliff Morrison," Jaclyn told Fran, "about six months ago. Unfortunately, Mike here has never gotten over it. For weeks he kept pestering me with midnight phone calls. Oh, Jaclyn, I want you back. Oh, Jaclyn, please. Everytime I broke up with somebody and started seeing somebody new it was always the same thing. Oh, please, Jaclyn. You're not seeing anyone now, take me back.

DEADLY DETENTION 167

Then when I started seeing Glen . . . Well! Mike here hated that most of all."

The cheerleader's eyes were on Mike again, boring into him, pinning him to the wall. "The night after my first date with Glen, the phone rings. He goes, 'It's me.' Then he goes, 'Tell me you're not going out with Davis.' I go, 'Yeah, I am.' He goes, 'I don't believe it! What do you want to hang out with that moron for? The guy's a retard.'"

"Did he really say that?" Glen asked, pained.

"Of course I didn't say that," said Mike. "This is all a total lie."

"You can deny it all you like," Jaclyn said. "But I've got a drawer full of your pathetic letters, all about your obsession."

"Those are old letters, Jaclyn," Mike said.

"Well I've got them," Jaclyn said. "And I'm sure the police won't think they're so old."

Mike tried to smile but his face was stiff with fear. "At least it's nice to know you saved them," he said.

"I saved them as evidence," Jaclyn said sharply. "Because I knew how sick you were, even then."

"He really called me a retard?" Glen said, his voice barely audible.

"He hates you so much he can hardly look at you," Jaclyn said.

"Hold it," Fran said. "Hold on." She had both hands up in the air, as if pleading for quiet and calm. "So you two used to go out," she said to Jaclyn. "But what does that have to do with anything? What does that have to do with Owen and Jill?"

Jaclyn gave Fran a cold look, as if she were annoyed at the interruption. "You haven't figured it out yet, Weber? Then maybe I am the smartest kid in the school, after all."

She looked back at Mike. "Me and Glen are the real targets," she said. "Aren't we?"

Mike didn't answer.

"Everyone knows how crazy Crowley's been acting these days," Jaclyn went on. "When they find the bodies tomorrow, everyone will think the same thing. Crowley blew his fusebox once and for all. Old Crowley went nutsy. That's why Mike had to kill Owen and Jill. And that's why he was going to kill you, too, Fran. Because he was going to pin this whole thing on Crowley the Crazy."

Fran shivered. "I don't believe that," she said. "That's too awful."

"But it's true, isn't it, Mike?" Jaclyn asked.

Mike still didn't answer. His head was down.

Glen started moving forward; he was holding his broken pointer in one hand, the jagged edge pointing toward Mike.

Mike turned to watch him come. "I didn't

do this," he insisted. "I swear to you on my mother's life, I—"

Glen kept coming.

And then—abruptly—Mike turned and ran.

Nineteen

Glen ran after him. So did Jaclyn. So did Fran.

They scattered through the school's dark hallways.

The deadly game of hide and seek ended twenty minutes later. It ended with horrible shrieks and groans from Mike.

His shouts signified that he'd been found.

The cries were coming from the second floor of the left wing of classrooms, just down the hall from the teachers' lounge. His wailing and whimpering went on for a long time.

Then the crying stopped.

A few minutes later, doors opened at either end of the dark hallway, and Jaclyn and Glen both rushed toward each other, converging in front of the open doorway to Crowley's lab. Fran arrived last, pushing into the doorway after them.

Glen flicked on the lights.

Crowley's lab was a long room lined with

green wooden experiment tables, which in turn were lined with metal stools. On the walls were charts showing how to dissect a frog; on the tables were the jars of frogs waiting to be cut up. In the far corners of the room, two life-size, see-through figures, one male, one female, watched over the room like guards. They hadn't done their guard duty very well.

Mike was lying facedown on the lab floor, a scalpel buried deep in the back of his neck. From the trail of blood he had left behind, it looked as if he had crawled partway around the room as he died.

There was a clatter as Glen dropped his pointer. He rushed forward, knelt, and turned Mike partway over. He stared at his face for a moment, then let the body turn back, facedown.

"Did you do this?" Glen asked Jaclyn. Tears glistened on his cheeks.

Jaclyn was looking down at Mike. She turned away, muttering, "Go to hell, Glen. Go straight to hell."

"Did you?" he shouted.

"NO!" Jaclyn shouted back. "Did you?"

Fran turned and looked at the blackboard. "Oh, no," she said. She said it so softly Jaclyn and Glen almost didn't hear her.

But then Glen, and then Jaclyn, looked to see what Fran was talking about. A message had been scrawled on the board in yellow chalk:

> Here's one last problem for all you stupid students.
> Jill, Owen, and Mike are dead.
> How many does that leave?

The note on the board was signed, "The Corporal."

Twenty

They all gaped at the board.
"Jaclyn?" Fran said at last.
Jaclyn turned from the blackboard to look at her.
"This kind of proves Mike was telling the truth, doesn't it?" Fran asked. "About those announcements?"
"Yeah," Jaclyn said. "I guess it does."
They were both sounding like zombies, Fran thought, as if they couldn't get any feeling into their words.
"So it was Crowley after all," Jaclyn said.
"What? But his car . . ." said Glen.
"That doesn't mean anything," Jaclyn said quickly.
She started pacing around the room, moving through the maze of experiment tables like a rat trapped in an experiment, a rat that kept receiving little electric shocks. "He must have parked in a *student* parking space," she said, chopping the air with her hands. "That was

so dumb of you, Weber. To just assume he had gone like that! Really stupid!"

"You thought it, too," Glen pointed out.

"Shut up!" Jaclyn said, clutching her head. "Shut up! Shut up! Shut up!"

"You're the only one who's talking," said Glen sullenly.

Jaclyn rushed at Glen, who was still kneeling beside Mike. She raised a hand as if to strike him. He cringed. But she lowered her hand, yelling instead, "You *fool!* Can't you understand? It's Crowley. He's out there. He killed Mike. And now he's going to kill us."

"You're sure?" Glen asked.

"Of course I'm sure!"

"Yeah? Well you were pretty sure just a little while ago that Crowley was gone," said Glen doggedly. "You were pretty sure that Mike was a—" He let the thought trail off, apparently not eager to say the word "murderer."

"Yeah, well I was wrong," Jaclyn said. She flexed her long, glossy red nails like tiger claws. "Okay. It's still three against one," she said. "Now we just need to find him."

"Find him?" Glen said. "No way."

"I'm not waiting around," Jaclyn said. "I'll go nuts. Maybe if we go out there we can sneak up on *him* for a change. And cut his heart out."

"No way," Glen said again. "We're staying here."

DEADLY DETENTION 175

"Oh," Jaclyn said. "And who put you in charge?"

"We're staying here," Fran agreed. She said it firmly, as if that would end the argument.

And it might have.

But just then—

At the end of the long hall . . .

The door to the teachers' lounge flew open with a loud bang.

Twenty-one

Jaclyn rushed out into the hall. Fran and Glen followed her.

At the end of the hall stood Mr. Crowley, his tall powerful body silhouetted by the light from the lounge. He started down the hall. He was carrying the empty whiskey bottle in one hand.

When he saw them, he stopped short. "What are you kids doing here?" he yelled.

The students didn't answer, just skittered backward, about to run. Crowley hurried toward them. They backed up some more, keeping the distance between them, occasionally turning their heads to see how far they had to go to get to the stairs.

"Where are you going?" Crowley yelled.

They kept backing up. They had their hands on each other's arms, as if trying to pull themselves away from the teacher's magnetic power. But then—

"Wait right there!" he suddenly ordered.

They all stopped short. It was a deeply ingrained instinct. Even after three gruesome murders, when a teacher yelled at you, you listened. You obeyed.

Crowley kept coming. "You kids are in a lot of trouble," he said. "What have you been up to around here, anyway? No good, I'm sure."

Jaclyn found her voice first. "You left us here!"

"We were locked in!" yelled Glen.

Crowley stopped and scratched his crew cut. Even from this distance, Fran could hear that *tsk* sound as he sucked on a tooth. He whistled. Then he laughed. "You were locked in? That's funny! Just like I always threatened you, huh?"

He seemed to be in a fine mood. "Well, that was Binder's fault, not mine. Guess he didn't know you were all still up there. Who would have thought . . . I had to rush out of here," Crowley explained. "A family emergency. Well, I thought it was a family emergency. Turned out to be some goddamn prank call. Anyway, I was sure you fools would all just go home." He laughed uneasily.

The students were all looking at each other in the dark—quick glances, not wanting to take their eyes off Crowley for too long. They were all asking each other an unspoken question. Was Crowley telling the truth? Or was this another trick?

"If you thought we just went home," Fran said, "then—" She paused, looking puzzled.

"Then what are you doing back here now?" Jaclyn called.

Crowley didn't answer. Just kept walking toward them.

And then—

It was hard to say who started to run first.

Was it Glen? Crowley?

Whoever it was, the sudden movement caused an instant stampede.

The three students turned and raced flat-out for the stairwell.

Right behind them, running hard, came the Corporal.

Twenty-two

Fran clattered down the stone steps. She was taking two, three, four steps at a time. She felt like she was flying through the air, she was running so fast. It was amazing to her that she didn't fall. It seemed like only the presence of Jaclyn and Glen, flying down the steps alongside her, kept her from crashing to her death against the cold cement floor.

Above her, the stairwell door clanged open a second time. And now Crowley was racing down the steps right behind them; his heavy shoes hit the steps so hard it sounded like machine gun fire.

With Glen leading, the three teenagers raced through the dark hall, then turned toward the center of the school, trying to lose themselves in the maze of hallways.

"STOP RIGHT NOW!" Crowley roared.

But his voice had receded into the distance. They were getting away.

Glen turned sharply right, pulling Fran's arm to make sure she turned as well.

He skidded to a stop in front of a door with a pebbled glass top. The glass was lettered THE LANTERN. He flung open the door, and grabbing Fran and Jaclyn, pulled them into the room along with him.

He didn't turn on the light, but there was just enough streetlight and moonlight filtering through the one window to light up the clutter within. Here were the large wooden desks, the bins of photos, the lightboard for studying slides, the easel where Glen and other students pasted up yearbook copy when it came back from the typesetter. Usually, it was a cozy room, a haven where students could hang out and get away from the watchful eyes of the Harrison faculty. It didn't seem like a cozy room now.

"Give me a hand with this," Glen whispered to the girls. Grunting under the strain, the three teenagers slid one of the heavy desks a foot to the right, so that it blocked the door. Then they slowly backed away.

"Why are you running?" they heard Crowley shout. But the shout was faint and far off. "Stop right now or you'll have detention for a week. You hear me? A month!"

Fran breathed a sigh of relief. She turned. Jaclyn turned at the same time, and their eyes settled on the same object—the black desk phone.

The next instant, the two teenagers were

DEADLY DETENTION 181

both lunging across the room. Jaclyn got to the phone first. She put the receiver to her ear, then pulled it away and yanked out the tiny earplug from her walkman, then put the receiver back to her ear again. She listened a moment.

Then she put the receiver back down slowly, as if she had just received the worst possible news. She shook her head to indicate to the other two that the line was dead.

Fran giggled, slapping her hand over her mouth to stifle the sound. Jaclyn gave her a sharp look, as if to say, "Are you nuts?"

Fran pointed at Jaclyn's ear, touching her own ear to indicate what she meant. She was laughing now, but silently, and without humor. "You're still . . . listening to music?" she whispered. "After everything . . ?"

"Hey! Get a grip!" Jaclyn grabbed Fran by the shoulders and shook her hard. She raised her hand to slap her too—but Glen caught her hand and held it.

Jaclyn wrenched her hand free. "Don't touch me!" she told him. She didn't bother to whisper. Crowley could be anywhere by now, anywhere in the huge, empty school. "Don't ever touch me. You're the worst!"

She stalked off to the far side of the room, near the light of the window. Fran stayed where she was. She looked at Glen, at Jaclyn.

The two teenagers were glowering at each other silently in the dark.

"What did *I* do?" Glen asked Jaclyn.

"What didn't you do?"

Glen said, "Name one thing."

"You accused me of murder," Jaclyn said. "That's one thing."

"Yeah," Glen said. "It is."

"What's that supposed to mean?"

Glen shrugged.

"We're supposed to be going out," Jaclyn said bitterly. "You're supposed to have some loyalty."

"Sorry," Glen said sincerely.

"Yeah. Well that's not all."

"What else?"

"You know."

"I don't."

"It's the same thing you've been doing," Jaclyn muttered. "All night."

"And what's that?"

"Flirting."

Fran's head jerked back toward Jaclyn. She couldn't help laughing again. "Jaclyn, really. That's what you're worrying about at a time like this?"

"Don't try to deny it," Jaclyn said. She said it straight to Glen, as if Fran didn't exist. "I'll kill you if you try to deny it."

"So what if I've been flirting?" Glen asked. "You were flirting with Mike."

DEADLY DETENTION 183

"Guys," Fran said. "I hate to break this up. But there's a maniac out there roaming the halls, trying to find us and kill us and—"

The look on Jaclyn's face made Fran stop mid-sentence. "What?" Fran asked.

Jaclyn was staring at Glen, and there was horror in her eyes. "You!" she breathed.

"Oh, please," Glen said. "Don't even start. I've had it with these games. I really—"

"Fran," Jaclyn said, "I just figured it out."

"We've heard that before," Glen said.

"I think Crowley was telling the truth," Jaclyn said. "He's not the killer at all. It's Glen!"

"You really are amazing, you know that?" Glen said.

Fran was swiveling her head back and forth between the two, like a spectator at a tennis match. Suddenly Jaclyn lunged at Glen. She pushed him—or tried to. He caught her hands and she had to wrench them free again. Fran moved between them. "He'll hear us," she whispered fiercely. "C'mon. Stop it! Both of you."

Jaclyn backed off a few feet. "Look, Fran," she began, "there's something you should know. Last week I told Glen I wanted to break up."

"Oh, yeah, right," said Glen.

"Just let me finish," Jaclyn said sharply. "Then you can start your lying."

Glen rolled his eyes.

"I told him I wanted to break up," Jaclyn began again. "But he put up this incredible fight to talk me out of it. Begging me. Pleading with me not to dump him. So . . . I gave in."

"This is so totally—" Glen started.

"I know it was a mistake," Jaclyn rushed on. "The guy's a dumb jock and a sleazebucket. Real pond scum. But I figured if he was going to get *so* upset . . . it was easier to just keep going out with him. For now." She took a breath. "Anyway. This afternoon, we got into another big fight. We were in the music room. You know, our secret lunch makeout spot. So then he goes, 'Jaclyn, are you really serious about what you said? About us breaking up?' I go, 'Yeah. I am.' And the next thing I know he's storming around the room, swinging music stands around his head like a crazy man."

Glen put his hand over his mouth, as if that were the only way he could keep himself from interrupting this parade of lies.

Then Jaclyn's cold blue eyes widened. "Oh, my God," she said. "Fran, I just figured something out. That's *why* we got detention. It was all part of his plan."

"What plan?" Glen asked, as he hit his fist against his leg in frustration.

"Mrs. Johnson must have heard you yelling

DEADLY DETENTION 185

all the way from the library," Jaclyn said. "You *wanted* her to hear."

"I wasn't yelling. I raised my voice."

"You were yelling your head off."

"I wasn't. Mrs. Johnson just happened to come into the room. And the reason we got detention is because you weren't wearing any—"

Jaclyn clapped her hands together, loudly. "That's it! That's it! Fran, I'm a true genius. I've got it figured out now. It all fits, don't you see? I had the plan right, I just had the wrong killer."

"Jaclyn," Fran said as soothingly as she could, "we really gotta keep our voices down because—"

"Glen can't stand the idea that I'll be seeing other guys," Jaclyn said. She fingered the peace medallion around her neck, her pink tongue played around her red lips. "Can you, Glen?"

"Are you finished?" he asked.

"No, I'm not finished. Look at him, Fran. It's eating him alive. He's dying of jealousy. So then he comes up with this whole crazy scheme to—Oh, God!" She slapped her forehead. "I just can't believe it! Glen, I thought I knew you! And you're just like this, this *monster.*"

"What scheme?" Glen asked levelly.

"You were going to kill me and make it look

like the Corporal did it," Jaclyn said. She pursed her lips and gave Glen a nasty look, but the truth was, the cheerleader looked very close to tears.

"That is such crap," Glen said.

"Pretty amazing plan." Jaclyn whistled as if in admiration. "Wow, Glen, maybe you're not as brain-dead as I thought! But tell me this. What are you going to do now that Crowley's back?"

Glen stared at her in the darkness, not moving, not answering.

"Well that's easy, I guess," Jaclyn said. "You'll kill him, too. Right, Glen? Make it look like a murder-suicide."

The handsome athlete shook his head sadly. "Jaclyn, I should have realized it long ago," he said.

Jaclyn stopped her pacing. "Realized what?"

Glen plunged his hands deep into the pockets of his brown corduroy jacket; he hung his head slightly. When he spoke, his words seemed to be directed at the floor. Unlike Jaclyn, he spoke softly. "Fran, this is kind of obvious, I guess. But Jaclyn here is the vainest girl I've ever met."

Jaclyn made a hissing sound. Glen raised his eyes to hers, as if to say, You had your chance.

"I'm sure that's no surprise to you," Glen went on. "But you know what, Fran? I never knew, I never really knew it until just now."

"Knew what?" Jaclyn cried.

Glen's brown doe-eyes looked incredibly sad. He looked straight at Jaclyn as he said, "I never knew just how crazy you really are."

Jaclyn's mouth fell open. She made a "huh" sound, as if she were about to laugh. Then she said, "What are you trying to pull? This is another part of your plan, isn't it? *Isn't it?*"

"You're nuts, Jaclyn," Glen said simply, and there was still that sadness in his face. "You're certifiable."

"You try to kill five kids and a teacher and you call me nuts? Ha!"

"Fran?" Glen said.

Nervously, Fran kept pushing her dark-brown hair back behind her ear. When she answered, her voice was as hushed as Glen's. "Yeah?"

"Can I ask you something?"

The way he said it—so simply—made Fran hold her breath.

"Has any guy ever broken up with Jaclyn, as far as you know?"

They both turned to look at the cheerleader. She was standing a few feet away, her blue eyes gleaming, her teeth almost bared.

"No," Fran said. "As far as I know, no one ever has."

She squinted across the dark room at Glen, as if trying to see the point he was driving at.

"Never ever, right?" Glen asked.

Fran shrugged her shoulders.

"That's right. And everybody knows it," Glen said. "Every kid at Harrison knows that Jaclyn is always the one that does the dumping, and not the other way around. No one would ever break up with Miss Popular, because then she wouldn't be Miss Popular, now would she?"

Glen looked at Jaclyn. So did Fran.

"Stay away from him, Fran," she warned. "He's a killer."

"Do you know what it would do to Jaclyn if someone dumped her first?" Glen asked. "It would destroy her."

"Don't listen to him!" Jaclyn said.

"It's true what Jaclyn says. Most of it. She did talk about breaking up with me today." Glen was leaning back against one of the desks. He looked down at his sneaker as he used it to crush a piece of photographic paper that had fallen there. "And you want to know why, Frannie?"

Fran's voice was almost inaudible. "Why?"

She knew the answer that was coming an instant before she heard it. It still stunned her.

"She wanted to break up with me because I told her I've got this wicked crush on you."

There was a profound silence in the room, as if all sound had suddenly been sucked out

DEADLY DETENTION

along with the air, plunging them into a perfect vacuum. Glen gave Fran a tiny smile. "That's why," he said.

Fran almost laughed. Anything to break that silence. "Ah," she said at last, not knowing what to say and feeling like a total idiot.

"You're going to pay," Jaclyn warned Glen.

"Did you hear what I said?" Glen asked Fran.

"Yeah." She could no longer meet his gaze. She started chewing her already badly bitten nails.

Jaclyn laughed. "You see how sick he is, Fran? He's in the middle of trying to kill all of us, and he's like, what? Asking you out on a date?" She laughed hysterically.

"I'm not asking her out," Glen said, his jaw jutting out in anger.

"Why not?" Jaclyn said. She started circling around him again. "I thought you said you had such a crush on her!"

"I'm not asking her out *right now,*" Glen corrected himself. He didn't look at Fran when he said it, but right then, right in the middle of everything, Fran felt herself blushing bright red with embarrassment.

Jaclyn's next move was lightning quick. With a hiss, she snapped her hand out, her long red nails raking across Glen's cheek before he could grab her hand.

Glen put his hand to his face, then to his

mouth, tasting the blood. "See how crazy she is, Fran?" he asked. "See how mad she gets?"

Blood wasn't the only thing trickling down his cheek. There were tears now as well. "Every time I try to end it, Fran, she goes berserk. She says I begged her to stay with me. That's all in her head. She's the one begging. She threatens me, too. Says she'll kill me. Before tonight, though, I never knew she really meant it."

He met Jaclyn's eyes. "You're always saying I'm so dumb, Jaclyn," he said. "Maybe I am. I could never have thought of this whole murder plan like you did. That's how you figured out what the plan was, though, wasn't it? Because it was your plan all along."

"Shut up!"

"You want to know something even more crazy? I'm not mad at you. Not even after you killed Owen and Jill and Mike. Because I think I understand you, Jaclyn."

"You couldn't understand a first-grade Weekly Reader," Jaclyn scoffed. "It's true, Fran. Other than math, the guy is like a total—"

"My parents couldn't care less about me," Glen said. "They really couldn't. I mean, I was just a mistake, you know. To them I'm just some extra bills they don't want to pay. But I think I've got it easy compared to you, Jaclyn. If I had a mother like you do," Glen said,

"I'd go berserk." He spoke softly, but the words seemed to stop Jaclyn cold.

"Her mother's a lunatic," Glen told Fran. "A total basket case."

"Don't you dare talk about her!"

"She lives through her daughter. What's that word? From English class? Mr. Santana always uses it. Vic something."

"Vicarious?" Fran asked.

"Yeah. Victorious. Vicarious. Whatever. That's her mother, man. I'm telling you. If Jaclyn wasn't the most popular girl at Harrison, it would kill Jaclyn. But it would hurt her mom even worse."

Jaclyn was shrieking. "That's a lie! Lie! Lie! Lie!"

"Glen, I'm beginning to think everybody's parents are crazy," Fran said quietly. "But that doesn't mean that Jaclyn is a killer."

"She is," said Glen, and the finality with which he said it sent chills down Fran's spine.

"Glen," Fran said. "You're trying to tell me that Jaclyn would kill five kids? All to keep you from breaking up with her? I mean, do you really believe that?"

"Yeah. I do." He was looking at Jaclyn again. "But it looks like your plan didn't work. 'Cause I'm breaking up with you right now. As of this moment. So, you can kill me, you can do whatever you want, but it won't change the truth of what happened. We're history, Jaclyn."

Jaclyn reached down into the arm of her jacket. Glen tensed, as if he expected her to pull out a weapon. But instead there was a tiny click as she turned on her walkman.

Glen chuckled. "You can try to hide in your music, Jaclyn, it won't do any good." To Fran, he said, "You don't believe she could kill? Just listen to what she listens to all day. Motorhead. 'Hellraiser.'"

Jaclyn nodded her head to the music and gave Glen a tiny wave. "Can't hear you," she said.

Glen ran both hands through his short hair, then used his hands to prop up his forehead. He looked miserable. "Miss Popular," he said to Fran. "You would think she would like herself, wouldn't you? But that's why she's always so nasty and bitchy to everyone. She hates herself most of all."

Abruptly, Jaclyn raised both hands in front of her, her fingers crooked like claws. But then her face began to work, and her hands slowly lowered. She was crying.

"You're such . . . a liar," she sobbed.

Neither Fran nor Glen moved. They just stood there as if paralyzed. As if the sight of Jaclyn Peeters crying was the most shocking thing they'd seen that night.

As abruptly as the tears began, they stopped. Jaclyn wiped her face briskly and smiled cheerfully. "All better," she said. Her mascara had smeared around her eyes, making big dark circles like the eye sockets of a skull.

"Guys," Fran said softly. "You want to know what I think? I think you're both crazy. It's Crowley."

"No," Jaclyn said matter-of-factly. "It's Glen."

"It's Jaclyn," Glen said. "And I can prove—"

He didn't finish his sentence.

Because just then they all heard the footsteps coming down the hallway.

They were coming right toward them.

Twenty-three

No one moved. But they were all breathing so hard that Fran was sure the sound would give them away.

The footsteps grew louder. Louder.

And then Crowley's hulking shadow passed—ghostlike—right in front of the pebbled glass of the door.

The shadow stopped.

So did Fran's heart.

He was right outside now, looking in.

But you couldn't see anything through that pebbled glass. Especially with the lights off.

Finally, the shadow moved on.

The footsteps grew softer and softer.

He had passed them by.

Fran let out a long sigh and moved to a nearby desk, bracing herself with one hand. "That was close," she said.

"I should have yelled something," Jaclyn said.

"Why didn't you?" Glen asked. "Since you're so sure I'm it."

"I should have."

Jaclyn had regained some of her composure, but her pale cheeks were still wet with tears. "My eyes must look just peachy," she said in her chipper voice. She started opening and closing drawers. "You don't happen to have a mirror on you, do you, Fran?" She flashed Fran a tiny smile, as if nothing had gone wrong, as if there weren't three teenagers lying around the school, dead.

"No," Fran said. "I don't."

Jaclyn opened more drawers, poking through the piles of photos and junk inside.

"Look at her," Glen said. "See what I mean? Three kids dead. She's worrying about her makeup."

"That's right," Jaclyn said into an open drawer. "Keep it up."

As if to punctuate her statement, she shoved a drawer shut. Holding her head high and whistling tunelessly, she brushed right past Glen. She yanked open the gray metal filing cabinet.

Then she gasped.

She backed up so hard she bumped into Glen.

She moved fast, past Glen to Fran. She was clutching Fran's arm, pointing.

"What is it?" Fran asked, gulping. "What?"

Glen's head spun to see what Jaclyn was

pointing at. He stepped toward the cabinet. He reached inside.

He pulled out a large metal cleaver, stained red with fresh blood.

He held the cleaver up near his head.

From the way he was holding it, it looked as if he was doing one of two things.

Either he was showing the weapon to Fran and Jaclyn.

Or he was getting ready to chop their heads off.

"Now how did this get here?" he asked.

Twenty-four

Fran got to the door first, frantically pulling on the doorknob. But the door wouldn't open. The barricade!

Jaclyn slammed into the desk with all her might, shoving it back. Then Fran yanked the door open. They ran.

Past the cafeteria. Past the library. Past the principal's office.

Fran turned her head only once to see if Glen was following them. It didn't look like he was. She didn't slow down, though. Neither did Jaclyn.

Finally, the pain in Fran's side grew too intense. She slowed to a halt, gasping for breath.

"Where—do—we—" Fran asked. She was breathing through her mouth, unable to finish the question.

Jaclyn looked both ways. "I . . . don't know!"

"He could be anywhere," Fran whispered. Her body was as tense and alert as a deer in a forest when it hears the twig-snap of an approaching hunter.

"Who?" Jaclyn asked.

"Crowley."

"What about Glen?"

"He could be anywhere, too. C'mon!" Fran seized Jaclyn's arm and pulled her toward the large pink door a few yards away. The girls' bathroom.

They hurried inside without turning on the lights. Both girls knew the place just as well in the dark. Like every other girls' room in Harrison High, the room was a long rectangle with a tiny vestibule of an entrance area. The floor and the bottom half of the bathroom's walls were done in pink tile. Pink sinks lined one whole wall, pink metal stalls lined the other. The pinkness of the decor did nothing to make the rooms less grim or prison-like.

Harrison girls had contributed their own decorations over the years, scratching all sorts of obscenities into the metal of the stalls and the white plaster of the upper walls. Even in the dark, Fran could probably have pointed to the spot on the wall where a girl had written, "Mr. Franklin sucks eggs," along with an obscene diagram.

They stood stock still. Jaclyn grabbed Fran's hand and squeezed it. They listened for footsteps outside the bathroom. Heard none.

Jaclyn let go of Fran's hand and moved to the sink, turning the spigot just enough to run a silent trickle of water. She washed her face, drying it with paper towels.

"Glen's going to get the electric chair for this," she said. She tossed the paper towels on the floor. "You watch. They'll try him as an adult and they'll kill him."

"Jaclyn, for the hundredth time, I don't think Glen—"

"You think it's Crowley, I know. But you're wrong." Jaclyn sighed, the raggedy sigh of a girl who had recently been crying.

She turned and looked at Fran. Fran was hugging herself with her long arms, rocking back and forth on the balls of her feet, crying softly. "We're never going to get out of here," Fran said.

Jaclyn chuckled, tossing her head in a show of bravado. "Sure we will. It's just going to be in body bags, that's all."

Fran laughed through her tears. "You're sick, you know that?"

Jaclyn crossed to the wall, pulled down another paper towel and blew her nose. "Let me ask you something, Weber. Do you really enjoy your life so much, that you're so afraid to die?"

"Uh huh. I do."

"Well, I don't," Jaclyn said. She smiled. "I hate my life."

Fran's green eyes met the ice-blue eyes of the cheerleader. "Why? I mean, you've got it all. Looks, brains, every kid in the school wishes they—"

"Yeah, well, Glen's right," Jaclyn said matter-of-factly. "I do hate myself, if you want to know the truth."

"That's too bad."

Jaclyn laughed, looked away. "Frannie the shrink," she said. "That's what people call you, you know."

"Yeah, I know."

"Yeah, well, Glen was right. Except the part about me killing those guys. That was the only lie. Wait here."

"Where are you going?"

"I've got to pee."

"Now?"

"No," Jaclyn said. "I had to pee about six hours ago. But this is the only chance I've gotten."

"Jaclyn, Crowley could come in here any minute."

"Then I'll die peeing, but if I don't pee, I'll die."

Fran was still crying, but now she was also giggling. She saw the shadow that was Jaclyn move toward one of the stalls, saw the pink metal door swing outward, then shut again. Heard the tiny bolt on the door rattle shut.

"You think this bolt would save me if Glen comes in here?" Jaclyn asked quietly.

"No."

Fran leaned back against the sink, her left hand holding her right elbow behind her back.

"Hey, Weber."

"What?"

"You mind turning on that faucet a little harder? It helps me go."

Fran smiled. "Sure." She turned the spigot to a steady stream. She waited. "C'mon, Peeters," she said. "Don't take all day, I'm getting scared standing out here by myself."

"Don't *you* have to go?"

"Nah. I think I went in my pants about two hours ago."

Now it was Jaclyn's turn to giggle. Fran groped through the darkness, found one of the many empty stalls, closed the toilet seat and sat down. She was utterly exhausted. Even though her adrenaline was surging and her heart was pounding, she was worn out. If she closed her eyes, she felt like she might sleep for a week.

The bathroom was clammy. There was the smell of human excrement in the air, which Mr. Binder's daily moppings never fully erased. But there was a stronger, more dominant stench in the room. Cigarette smoke.

"Can you believe Jill got caught for smoking?" Fran asked.

"I know," Jaclyn said from a few stalls away. "That girl had about the worst luck in history."

It was a known fact at Harrison that all the kids went to the bathrooms to smoke. Rather than make the entire student body stay after school every day, the teachers always looked the other way.

Jaclyn snickered. "I hate to say it, but it figures for someone like Berman. She started smoking two weeks ago. So, wham!—right away she gets caught."

"She got more than caught," Fran said hollowly.

Jaclyn giggled harder. "Yeah. I guess you could say smoking really took years off her life!"

Fran tried not to laugh. She failed. The exhaustion, all she had been through, it was too much. She started to laugh so hard she shook. She had to clap both hands over her mouth to keep the sound from coming out. And the more she tried not to laugh, the harder she guffawed.

It felt like she would never be able to stop laughing again.

She was wrong about that.

DEADLY DETENTION 203

Because at that second, something happened that stopped her laughing instantly.

The bathroom door opened.

The lights flicked on.

Twenty-five

Silently, but quickly, Fran closed her stall door. There was no lock on this stall. The metal bolt and hasp had been pried off, leaving only four rusty holes. She closed the door all the way. Then thought better of it, and opened it several inches. She put her feet up on the edge of the toilet, wrapping her arms around her legs.

Through the hinge of the door she could see a tiny vertical slice of the brightly lit bathroom. Through that slice now walked Crowley. "You girls in here?" he growled.

He moved to the sink. The sink that was still on. He looked down at it for a moment, then shut it off. "Peeters?" he called. "Weber? Berman?"

He moved out of Fran's line of vision. She heard him opening a stall door. From the sound of it, he had opened the very first stall, the one by the entrance. "I'm getting sick of looking for you girls. I really am. You're all going to be expelled, no matter how long you

DEADLY DETENTION 205

hide, so you might as well come out now and face the music."

He opened the next stall door.

And the next.

And then he opened the stall door right next to Fran's.

She squeezed her legs tighter, holding her breath.

She was looking down. In the gap below the pink metal of her own stall door, she could see the teacher's scuffed black wingtips. He was standing right in front of her stall.

She waited for the door to fly open.

It didn't.

"Crazy brats," Crowley muttered. "I'll kill them. I'll kill every last one of them."

Fran shivered.

And then the heavy wingtips were moving again, back the way they had come.

The lights flicked off.

And a minute later, Jaclyn pulled open Fran's stall in the darkness. "Let's go," she whispered.

Fran didn't put her feet down or come out of her tight ball.

"Go where?"

"We've got to find a way out."

Fran shook her head. "There's no way."

"So what do you want to do? Stay here until he comes back?"

"Maybe he won't come back. Why would he look in here again?"

"He's going to look everywhere," Jaclyn said. "We've got to go."

Fran's green eyes strained to make out Jaclyn's face. "Are you smiling?" she asked.

"Yeah."

"Why?"

"Don't you see what I'm saying? I'm saying you're right. It's Crowley. You win."

Fran didn't answer, didn't move.

"You heard him, didn't you? He's the killer."

"I'm not going," Fran said.

Jaclyn sighed. "C'mon," she said. "It's our only chance. Besides, you can't stay in here. I just stunk up the joint."

That did it. Fran finally smiled. Jaclyn reached out a hand. Fran took it.

They made their way to the door. Jaclyn pinched Fran's arm.

"What's that for?"

"Just to see if I'm dreaming," Jaclyn said.

Fran laughed again. "You're supposed to pinch yourself, not me."

"No way. I'm not stupid."

Smiling, Jaclyn opened the door.

Crowley lunged right at them.

Twenty-six

"Gotcha!" Crowley yelled, "you little—"

Shouting with terror, both girls jumped backward. It was pure instinct, pure terror; it was also a good move. As the teacher came lunging toward them, Jaclyn was able to duck down, so that she went right under his outstretched arm.

Crowley turned to grab her. He caught a handful of her orange cheerleading jacket—but the jacket came off in his hands. At the same time, Fran shoved Crowley from behind. He crashed into the tiled wall with a loud thud. But he bounced off and reached for Jaclyn as she ran.

This time he caught some of her wavy blond hair. She screamed, her head flinging back so fast it seemed for sure it would come off.

But now Fran attacked Crowley's arm. The arm that held Jaclyn's hair and also blocked her own escape. Without thinking, she sunk her teeth into his bare flesh.

He howled in pain. He also let go of Jaclyn.

She fell to her knees, but scrambled up again almost at once.

Jaclyn ran. She rounded the corner, picking up speed as she found her footing on the waxy floors.

She rounded another corner, and raced halfway down the next hall.

Only then did it occur to her that Fran wasn't right behind her.

She slid to a halt, screaming, "Frannie!"

There was no answer.

She screamed once—twice more. Then she turned and kept running.

Twenty-seven

It was almost fifteen minutes before Jaclyn and Fran ran into each other again, in the hallway outside the library. They hugged. "Oh, God, I thought he got you," Jaclyn whispered.

"He almost did!"

"Oh, you got away! You got away!" She squeezed Fran so hard she couldn't breathe. Finally, she let go. Fran whispered, "Where's Glen?"

"I don't know. And I don't care."

"Well you better care," Fran said.

"Why?"

"Because Glen is the killer."

"Fran? Are you insane? Crowley just tried to kill us."

"No, he didn't. He tried to catch us. There's a difference."

"Oh, yeah. And what do you think he's going to do to us after he catches us? Make us write 'We were bad girls' on the board a hundred times? Give me a break!"

Her clothes torn, her body slumping with

exhaustion, Fran leaned up against the gray wall of metal lockers. Then she looked to the right—and almost screamed. There was a pair of eyes staring out at her through the horizontal slats of the locker door.

Fran covered her mouth. Then she looked more closely. It wasn't a pair of eyes. It was just the metal of a student's spiral notebook, glinting as it reflected the yellow safety lights in the hall.

"What?" Jaclyn hissed. "What is it?"

"I thought someone was hiding in the locker," Fran said. She breathed deeply, or tried to. "We've got to find Crowley," she said.

"Why?"

"Because he can help protect us against Glen."

"Fran, you're mental, you know that?"

"You're the one who thought it was Glen. You accused him."

"I was wrong."

"Listen," Fran said. "Think back. What did Crowley say in the john?"

"He said he was going to kill every last one of us. So far, he's doing a pretty good job of it."

"That's what he always says," Fran said. "Day in and day out. No, I meant when he first came in."

As terrified as Jaclyn looked, there was excitement in her eyes now, the excitement of a sleuth about to solve a puzzle. "He called out our names," she said. Though she was whispering, she still managed to imitate Crowley's voice. "You girls in here?" she called. "Peeters? . . . Weber? . . ."

They said the last name together. *"Berman."*

The two girl's were only inches apart. Fran could feel the cheerleader's hot breath on her neck. "He doesn't know she's dead," Jaclyn said.

"Because he didn't kill her," Fran said.

Jaclyn thought for a moment. "Let's scream till Crowley finds us."

"No!"

"Why not?"

"Because Glen could find us first." Fran looked nervously around the hallway. "Here, maybe the library's open."

"You want to catch up on your reading?"

"I thought I might," Fran said. "Since I've got a little time on my hands. After all," she opened the library door, "tomorrow's a school day."

Jaclyn stepped inside first, followed closely by Fran.

They walked right into Glen, who fell on them with the cleaver.

Twenty-eight

He kept falling. His body had been propped up behind the door. He now fell to the floor. There was a letter opener in his back. Only the gold handle was visible. The knife was stuck through a note.

Fran moaned and fell to her knees beside Glen's body. She pulled the knife out. She had to wiggle the handle to do it, but she did it.

She picked up the note. It read, "You don't have a clue, do you?"

Crying softly, she rolled Glen over. It was a struggle. He seemed to weigh an awful lot now that he was dead. But his heart-shaped face was as handsome and soft and gentle as ever. His brown doe-eyes were open, staring up at her sadly. A trickle of dark, red blood had run down from his full lips, down through the handsome cleft in his chin.

She looked away, covering her mouth with her hand.

She found herself looking at Jaclyn's legs in

their black shimmery tights. She slowly lifted her gaze, up the legs, past the crinkly, vinyl, light-green skirt, the lacy white blouse. Up to the blond girl's head.

Jaclyn was staring straight down at her, a crazy smile playing across her pretty features. "There goes your little theory, huh?" Jaclyn asked.

Fran stood quickly, backing up a few steps. She was shivering madly now. "Oh, my God!" she said.

Then she turned and bolted.

Jaclyn raced after her, yelling, "Wait! It's not me! Fran! Wait! Watch out for Crowley! Fran!"

Fran didn't wait. She ran straight for the old wooden door that led down to the basement. But Jaclyn turned the corner just in time to see her disappear through the doorway. "Wait!" she yelled again. Then she slowed to a walk.

Fran had slammed the basement door shut behind her. Jaclyn turned the knob slowly, carefully, then yanked open the door. The stairway was deserted. Jaclyn started down the steps.

The basement was dark and smelled of dust. There was just enough light seeping in through the tiny windows near the basement's ceiling to reveal the blurred shape of the huge boiler. Overhead was a maze of large pipes wrapped with thick insulation padding, like huge bandaged limbs.

Still smiling that crazy smile, Jaclyn groped her way forward. Her foot clanged into a metal bucket.

At the same moment, something smacked her hard right in the face.

She stepped back sharply, then groped in the dark for what had hit her. She felt it with her hands. It was the long wooden handle of Binder's old mop.

"Fran?" Jaclyn whispered. "Frannie? Frannie Weber! Please come out! You and Glen were right. We're only safe if we stick together."

Even as she said the words, though, her hands were quietly closing around the mop's wooden handle. She lifted the mop from the bucket. She hoisted it over her head, ready to swing the wooden handle like a bat.

Her face was crazed with fury and concentration. But there was only sweetness in her voice as she whispered, "C'mon, Fran, I can't see a thing. I'm going to kill myself here. Show me where you are."

Then she heard something move. It was just around the corner.

She edged forward in the darkness, gripping the broom handle more and more tightly.

Around the corner, there was light.

She raised the wooden handle high in the air, ready to smash it down on Fran's head with all her might.

Twenty-nine

Jaclyn turned the corner hard, springing forward. Then she froze. She opened her mouth to scream. No sound came out—just a tiny choking sound. Her hands let the mop drop to the cement floor.

Sitting in a pool of blood, his eyes still open, breathing his last, was Mr. Crowley.

Or what was left of him.

The right side of his head had been blown off.

"So you finally figured it out," said Fran from behind her. "Too late." She pulled the trigger.

Jaclyn straightened as the first bullet hit, as if she were coming to attention. She was falling before the second bullet struck.

Fran calmly wiped off the gun with a rag she had found in the basement. Using the rag to avoid leaving any fingerprints, she placed the gun in Crowley's right hand.

"You got that part right," Fran told Jac-lyn's corpse. "I am going to make it look like a murder-suicide. See?" She held up a suicide note, as if Jaclyn's dead body could take a look. Then she slipped the note inside the pocket of Crowley's greasy gray pants.

"I've got to say, killing Crowley was the only pleasure I've had tonight," said Fran grimly. "After the way he treated me. And you. All of us. Killing him was a real pleasure."

She looked down at Crowley's slumped body, her face red with hatred. "Bastard," she said. "People like you. It's all your fault!"

She backed away. She suddenly didn't want to look at Jaclyn. It was Jaclyn who had thrown up in the cafeteria. Fran had been surprised and grossed out when she saw that some of the vomit had caught the edge of her shoe. But she now felt as if she might throw up as well, that she definitely would throw up if she looked at the young cheerleader. It had felt good to kill Crowley. But Jaclyn—

Fran turned, and moving as quickly as she could through the darkness, started making her way back upstairs. For God's sake, she told herself. She had done the whole thing so beautifully. She ought to give herself at least a few minutes to enjoy her success before she started picking herself apart.

That's what her parents would do, of course. They'd pick her apart. The moment she made any accomplishment or achievement, they'd immediately start with the criticism. It was never perfect, never enough.

Well, this—tonight—this was perfect. She had done everything right.

At least, it was going to be perfect. She still had a few details to attend to. First stop was the teachers' lounge.

As she made her way to the second floor, she indulged in a little gloating. Everything had gone according to plan.

She had gotten the idea one day in class, when Crowley was threatening to lock them in the school overnight. The words had seemed to stick in her brain; they never let go. She had thought about the plan for weeks.

Step one. Making sure they all got detention. That had been easy. Dampening the spark plugs in Mike's car. Tattling on Jill after *giving* her a new pack of cigarettes. Adding that extra page to Owen's term paper, the one with all the dirty words. Giving away Glen's and Jaclyn's secret makeout spot in the music room. And simplest of all: getting herself sent to detention, by stealing Beth Corn's wallet.

In the teachers' lounge, Fran sifted through the trash, unfolding the crumpled pink balls of message slips until she found the one she was looking for. She had written out the message for Crowley herself when he sent her to get the water. The message had said that his son had been arrested. Crowley was always willing to be-

DEADLY DETENTION 219

lieve the worst about any kid, his son most of all.

Pocketing the note, she took one last look around the teachers' lounge. Then she flicked the light off with her elbow and headed upstairs.

It was a pretty amazing feeling. After weeks of planning, to have everything go so well, just as she had envisioned it. There were so many times when things could have gone wrong. Like when Jill had that anxiety attack. She could have blown the whole thing right there. Fran had probably been more panicked than Jill!

But in the end, everything had fallen into place.

Fran felt so light-headed she thought she might faint.

Of course, Mike's prank, when he impersonated Crowley on the P.A. system, that was a stroke of luck. She couldn't take credit for that. But everything else went according to plan.

Back in Room #301, she found her backpack and looped the strap over one shoulder. Then she carefully erased her name from the bottom of the list of names on the board. She smiled as she looked at the remaining names.

With her only real competition now out of the way, she was sure she would win that Walton math prize. Her picture in the paper, the trophy—that would be just the thing she needed to get into Yale. That ought to shut her mother up once and for all!

Her smile broadened as she clomped down the stairs to the first floor. Her victims were all a little better than she was in math. But they weren't really as smart as she was, were they? No one had figured it out. Except Jaclyn, and she hadn't caught on until the very end.

It was like a math problem, in a way. What did all the kids have in common? If the others had looked at it that way, maybe they would have seen it coming. None of them usually got detention, except for Mike. Jill, Owen, Jaclyn, Fran—it was their very first time. That should have been their first clue. That should have started the wheels turning. Crowley had said it flat out. "You guys are supposed to be the smartest of the smart."

Well, Fran couldn't really blame them for not coming up with the solution. After all, her acting job had been brilliant, better than she had ever done in any play on any stage. She had believed in her part totally. And real tears—several times she had been surprised to find real tears pouring out of her eyes. She was going to win an Oscar someday. No doubt about it.

But then—for the first time that night—the old nagging criticisms started up again. That voice in her head. Her mother's voice. Had she *really* been acting? After all, she had been really scared, that wasn't fake. And she was really sorry to see the other kids die. That was real, too. Because she was fond of these kids. Jill, Owen, Mike—

No, she couldn't let herself think about that, not now. Not until later. Not until she was safe.

She stopped at the exit door and fumbled in her pocket for the master key she had "borrowed" from the principal's office this morning.

She let herself out.

The icy air felt refreshing after the hard night's work.

She shivered, as she had so often this day. And for the same reason. Not from the cold air. Not from fear. She shivered out of sheer amazement and pleasure, shivered with the thrill of it. She was really going to pull this off.

If only she could tell her mom how clever she'd been. That would spice up one of their heart-to-heart talks, now wouldn't it? Frannie the shrink. For once, maybe her mother would let her get a word in edgewise about her own life.

Fran smiled bitterly. Mrs. Weber would be pleased by the news. After all, every day she was begging Fran to get involved with more afterschool activities.

* * *

Fran's old Chevy chugged out of the Harrison High parking lot, leaving behind only a few stranded cars. Inside the large, dark school, five victims lay dead. One more was about to join the rest.

Jaclyn Peeters was lying on her back, her blue eyes wide open, glassy. Her own blood was pooled around her on the dusty floor.

She heard a click.

She smiled, ever so slightly. She had at least lived long enough to hear the walkman—which this last time she had set to *record*, not play—click off as the tape came to an end.

She licked her lips. Then she lay still, not smiling anymore, just repeating the comforting fact to herself over and over: She'd been taping since they went into the yearbook office. So, that meant she had taped Fran's confession.

She was sure of it.

Sure of . . .

Sure—

CLASSIC HORROR
From William W. Johnstone

__**Cat's Eye**   **$5.99**US/**$7.99**CAN
    0-7860-1000-2

__**Cat's Cradle**   **$5.99**US/**$7.99**CAN
    0-7860-1001-0

__**The Devil's Cat**   **$5.99**US/**$7.99**CAN
    0-7860-1005-3

__**The Devil's Kiss**   **$5.99**US/**$7.99**CAN
    0-7860-1003-7

__**The Devil's Touch**   **$5.99**US/**$7.99**CAN
    0-7860-1002-9

__**The Devil's Heart**   **$5.99**US/**$7.99**CAN
    0-7860-1004-5

__**Night Mask**   **$4.50**US/**$5.50**CAN
    0-8217-4743-6

Call toll free **1-888-345-BOOK** to order by phone or use this coupon to order by mail.

Name_____
Address_____
City _____ State _____ Zip _____
Please send me the books I have checked above.
I am enclosing $_____
Plus postage and handling* $_____
Sales tax (in New York and Tennessee only) $_____
Total amount enclosed $_____
*Add $2.50 for the first book and $.50 for each additional book.
Send check or money order (no cash or CODs) to:
Kensington Publishing Corp., 850 Third Avenue, New York, NY 10022
Prices and Numbers subject to change without notice.
All orders subject to availability.
Check out our website at **www.kensingtonbooks.com**

HORROR FROM PINNACLE...

__HAUNTED by Tamara Thorne
0-7860-1090-9 $5.99US/$7.99CAN

Its violent, sordid past is what draws bestselling author David Masters to the infamous Victorian mansion called Baudey House. Its shrouded history of madness and murder is just the inspiration he needs to write his ultimate masterpiece of horror. But what waits for David and his teenaged daughter at Baudey House is more terrifying than any legend; it is the dead, seducing the living, in an age-old ritual of perverted desire and unholy blood lust.

__THIRST by Michael Cecilione
0-7860-1091-6 $5.99US/$7.99CAN

Cassandra Hall meets her new lover at a Greenwich Village poetry reading—and sex with him is like nothing she's ever experienced. But Cassandra's new man has a secret he wants her to share: he's a vampire. And soon, Cassandra descends into a deeper realm of exotic thirst and unspeakable passion, where she must confront the dark side of her own sensuality ... and where a beautiful rival threatens her earthly soul.

__THE HAUNTING by Ruby Jean Jensen
0-7860-1095-9 $5.99US/7.99CAN

Soon after Katie Rogers moves into an abandoned house in the woods with her sister and her young niece and nephew, she begins having bizarre nightmares in which she is a small child again, running in terror. Then come horrifying visions of a woman wielding a gleaming butcher knife. Of course, Katie doesn't believe that any of it is *real* ... until her niece and nephew disappear. Now only Katie can put an end to a savage evil that is slowly awakening ... to unleash a fresh cycle of slaughter and death in which the innocent will die again and again!

Call toll free **1-888-345-BOOK** to order by phone or use this coupon to order by mail.

Name_____
Address_____
City_____ State _____ Zip _____
Please send me the books I have checked above.
I am enclosing $_____
Plus postage and handling* $_____
Sales tax (in NY and TN) $_____
Total amount enclosed $_____
*Add $2.50 for the first book and $.50 for each additional book.
Send check or money order (no cash or CODs) to: **Kensington Publishing Corp., Dept. C.O., 850 Third Avenue, New York, NY 10022**
Prices and numbers subject to change without notice. Valid only in the U.S.
All orders subject to availability.
Visit out our website at **www.kensingtonbooks.com**